if i tell

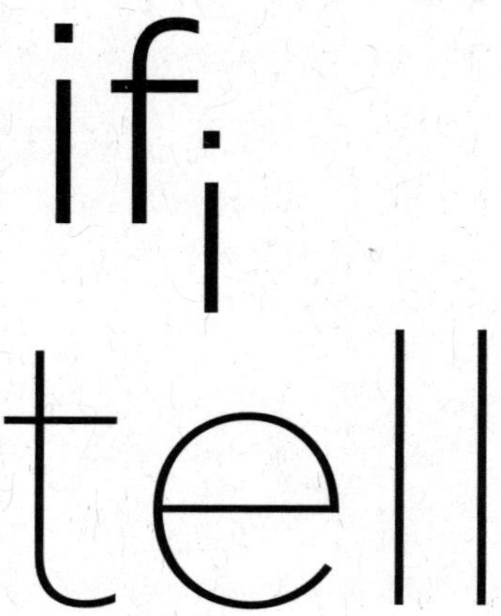

janet gurtler

Published by Sourcebooks Fire, an imprint of Sourcebooks, Inc.
P.O. Box 4410, Naperville, Illinois 60567-4410
(630) 961-3900
Fax: (630) 961-2168
teenfire.sourcebooks.com

Library of Congress Cataloging-in-Publication Data

Gurtler, Janet.
If I tell / by Janet Gurtler.
p. cm.
Summary: Raised by her grandparents, seventeen-year-old Jasmine, the result of a biracial one night stand, has never met her father but has a good relationship with her mother until she sees her mother's boyfriend kissing Jaz's best friend.
[1. Secrets—Fiction. 2. Conduct of life—Fiction. 3. Racially mixed people—Fiction. 4. Interpersonal relations—Fiction. 5. Grandparents—Fiction. 6. Washington (State)—Fiction.] I. Title.
PZ7.G9818If 2011
[Fic]—dc23

2011020272

Printed and bound in the United States of America.
VP 10 9 8 7 6 5 4 3 2 1

For the Mom and Tot group who saved me without knowing it:
Andrea Nicholas, Mydee Littauer, Sherri Barnes, Lara Jensen,
Victoria McLeod, and my ever-inspiring friend, Jana Joustra

chapter one

My heart raced as I stumbled down the steps. I needed to make sure I wasn't having a horrible hallucination, but I really wished that someone had spiked my soda and that drugs were distorting my reality. Like I was witnessing a train wreck, I wanted to look away but couldn't take my eyes off them.

Two people in a drunken clutch, their arms and legs pressed up against the wall. Two people who had absolutely no right to be locking lips—or any other body parts, for that matter.

I opened my mouth, but nothing came out. The only sound I could manage was an incoherent, panicky mumble. I turned and ran back up the stairs, pushing through a swarm of bodies until I was out of the house.

• • •

"Jaz." My mom's voice called my name and I jumped, spilling hot decaf mocha on my hand. Normally the fragrance of specialty coffees soothed me, but on this day Grinds smelled pretty much like burnt beans.

"Ouch! You okay? Sorry I startled you. It looks like you're in your own world back there."

"I'm fine." My hand stung, but I placed the coffee cup on the counter where the employees of Grinds arranged finished drinks like expensive steaming trophies. "Just working on a song in my head," I lied, shaking my scalded hand. "This decaf mocha is yours? It's not your usual caffeine fix."

"I know." She reached for the drink. "You and your song writing." She half smiled as she took a quick sip, then licked stray foam off her top lip. "We'll sit and chat before we go shopping?"

"Sure. Talk is cheap." I forced a smile of my own. I should have canceled and told her to go shopping without me. But I had to tell her what I'd seen. How could I not?

"Cheaper than this coffee anyway." She turned her head to search the café for an open table. "I'll find a seat. Grab a drink and join me when you're done, okay?"

She sashayed off without waiting for my answer, disappearing into the semi-full coffee shop. Grinds is our town's attempt to give Starbucks competition. Amber, the owner, hopes coffee will be her own personal lottery since Tadita is so close to Seattle.

I checked the clock. Five minutes until my shift ended. What I really wanted to do was bolt out the back door and jog home. That wouldn't mean breaking much of a sweat. I could crawl into my bed and pull the covers over my head before Mom noticed I'd left Grinds.

Sighing, I checked for new customers. No one approached the front counter with an urgent coffee craving, so I hurried to the back sink and shoved my hand under cold water to soothe the burn from the spilled coffee.

As I ran the water, a tall guy wearing a Grinds getup strolled through the employee door, tying the strings of an apron behind his back. Longish hair as black as charcoal brushed the shoulders of his white T-shirt. Hello, hot. Jackson Morgan, the new boy at Westwind High. Supposedly he'd failed kindergarten and had just gotten out of some school for delinquent boys. For dealing drugs. But I managed to stay composed when he nodded at me.

"Hey, Jaz. How's it going?" He sounded amused, as if he'd just remembered a good joke.

"Uh. Fine." He knew my name? He was in my English class, but like everyone else, he hadn't bothered to acknowledge my existence. Until now.

"Excellent." A pause. His mouth turned up in a crooked grin, and his eyes sparkled. "I'm fine too, by the way. Thanks for asking."

So much for composed. My cheeks burned and I studied my shoes, not sure how to reply. People generally didn't talk to me much. I never had to worry about what to say back.

"I'm just kidding." His voice was soft, almost apologetic, and I glanced up, noticing how nice and straight his teeth were.

"I know."

He was looking at me, his eyes narrowed like he was trying to figure something out. I blushed even more at the scrutiny. "No need to be shy. I don't bite."

I was torn between wanting him to leave me alone so I didn't have to come up with more to say and wanting him to keep talking. He'd already gone deeper than a lot of people did. Most kids at school assumed I was stuck-up. And that was almost better than shy. Shy made me feel like a failure. I took a step back and reached for my bracelet, rubbing the guitar charm Grandpa Joe had given me on my thirteenth birthday, right before he died.

"So was that your mom I saw you talking to?" Jackson glanced out at the seating area.

My gaze followed his. "Yeah. That's my mom." Bracing myself, I waited for the usual questions people asked when they saw my mom for the first time: Are you adopted? What color is your dad?

"Cool," he said. "Go ahead and do your thing. I can take care of stuff here. We can catch up later."

He made it sound like a promise. I tried to ignore the fluttering in my stomach. "You know what you're doing?"

It came out sounding like I was accusing him of some evil act. God. I was so not good at talking to boys. What I'd wanted to say was thank you for not being a jerk. Thank you for being nice. I filed the feeling. Maybe I could replicate it later in a song.

"Nope." He grinned. "But hey, I'll figure it out. Amber trained me. Monkey see, monkey do."

"Sorry," I mumbled. "I didn't mean it that way."

He twirled the hoop earring in his left ear. "I can handle it. No problem. Selling a *legal* drug, you know? Caffeine."

"Uh. Yeah." That seemed like a cue for me to say something about the rumors, but I was too chicken to go there.

He grinned again as if he'd read my mind. Hot. Definitely hot. I wondered if working at Grinds was part of his rehab or something.

He glanced toward my mom and I held my breath, praying he wouldn't slobber over her or say something obnoxious and ruin my impression of him.

"Your mom's pretty young," he said.

It sounded like an observation, not a crush.

"She's pretty blond too," I added.

"They say blonds have more fun," he quipped.

"She did when she was seventeen."

Mouth. Shut. Please.

He laughed, an interesting baritone sound. Almost musical. "That's how old she was when she had you?"

"Yup." I lifted my shoulder in a half-shrug.

"That's pretty young." He paused. "So? Is she cool?"

"My mom?"

He sounded as if he cared what I thought about her and not the other way around. It surprised me. *He* surprised me. "She's okay." I rolled my charm in my fingers. "I don't live with her." I frowned. I hadn't planned to tell him that. I don't usually advertise my weird family situation so freely. Even though in a town the size of Tadita, everyone pretty much knew already.

"I heard."

I waited, but he didn't say more. It didn't matter. People talked. They always did. He'd probably heard all the stories about me. Loner. Or loser. Depending on who was doing the telling. From someone at my high school, it had to be loser. So why was he being nice to me?

"I live with my grandma too," he said. He gestured his head toward the café. "Go talk to your mom. I got it covered."

"Thanks." I pulled off my stained blue apron and tossed it into the corner laundry bin as Jackson took over my shift. He lived with his grandma? Intrigued, I stared at him while he got to work.

Even a semi-awkward conversation with the school's newest bad boy beat joining my mom. Besides, who knew if the drug rumors were true. I vowed not to pay attention to gossip. He didn't appear to have labeled me based on what he'd heard.

He looked over and caught me watching, and my cheeks reheated. He grinned in a friendly way, but I quickly turned and pushed through the employee door.

I inhaled a deep breath as I made my way into the café. "Cherry, Cherry" by Neil Diamond piped in over the speakers—one of Grandpa Joe's favorite songs. At the thought of him, I forced my shoulders back.

Tell the truth, he'd have said. Always tell the truth.

Even if it meant breaking someone's world apart? The last thing in the world I wanted was intimate involvement with my mom's personal life, but I'd had a front-row seat. With binoculars.

Around the room, couples chatted at small, intimate tables. A group of girls giggled together, chairs and tables pushed up to each other. I stared at my mom as I approached her. A low-cut tank top peeked out from under her blazer. She liked to emphasize her amazing cleavage.

Another check on the long list of things I didn't inherit from her. Boobs. Nope. Blond straight hair. Nope. Coloring. Nope. I'm more a muddy mix of black and white. Mixing colors is pretty basic stuff for artists, but it's trickier with people.

"You look nice," I said as I sat. "You came straight from work?"

Her eyes widened. Oops. Normally I'd be more careful about pouring it on too thick, but she'd need it after what I had to tell her. And she did look nice.

She nodded. "Thanks." She lifted her mug and sipped her coffee. "I swear I'd almost prefer to wear a uniform like yours. So much easier."

I glanced at my smeared black pants and dingy white T-shirt, the lame Grinds uniform. "This?"

"Well. It's not expensive. And easy to coordinate. Besides you're so tall and slim, and with your coloring, you look good in anything you wear."

"My coloring makes me look cheap and easy?" I tucked my long legs under the table. Being around my glamorous and petite mom always made me feel like a clumsy giraffe.

"I said 'not expensive and easy to coordinate.' You're listening with marshmallows in your ears. You're beautiful." She grinned. "You're not having anything to drink?"

"I'm not thirsty."

"Lacey's not working?" Mom asked.

I glanced away. "No. A new guy is." I looked behind the coffee counter at Jackson. He was making a latte for a girl. She twirled blond hair around her finger and giggled as she chatted with him. She obviously had no problems with flirting.

"That's too bad," Mom said, and I focused back on her as her forehead wrinkled. The almost four-year age difference between Lacey and me didn't bother her. I think she was just glad I'd finally found a friend.

Mom didn't understand how I could go to school with the same kids for years and not have a gaggle of girls to gossip with. She'd had oodles of friends and dated the hottest football player at my age. But look what that had gotten her.

Me.

I'd never told her the truth about what happened to me and still wasn't even sure which one of us I was protecting.

"I thought Lacey might want to shop with us," Mom said. "The sales at the mall are supposed to be amazing. And she's so good at picking out bargains."

My underarms felt sticky with sweat. I sat up straighter. "Lacey is not coming." I didn't think we'd be shopping anyhow, but I didn't say that. Not yet.

Her expression softened. "No big deal. Just you and me is good." She leaned back, studying me. "Hey, I know what looks different about you. You don't have your guitar. You know, you look almost naked without it slung over your shoulder. "

"Why would I bring it shopping?" At the same time, I wished I'd brought it so I could clutch it to my chest like a kid with a teddy bear. My guitar was my most prized possession, and holding it gave me more comfort than I'd even realized until that moment.

Mom took another sip of her decaf, frowning at me over the top of her mug. "Is everything okay? You seem kind of…off."

I shrugged and stared at her coffee cup.

"How's Grandma?" she asked.

"Grandma?" I frowned and glanced up at her. "The same. Busy."

"Busy saving the world?" She sipped her coffee again and then placed the mug on the table. "You're happy with Grandma, aren't you, Jaz?"

My stomach did a backflip.

"No. No. Don't look so worried. I'm not going to ask you to move in with me and Simon again."

My stomach did a double flip then, and I swallowed hard, trying to block out an image of Simon. When Mom and Simon first moved in together years before, Mom asked me to move in with them, but Grandma and Grandpa fought her. I'd been glad no one made me choose then. I certainly didn't want to live with Mom and Simon now.

"Grandma would have a fit if I tried to take you away from her, especially with Grandpa gone."

I slumped down in my chair, wondering how she managed to read my mind so well sometimes. And other times, not at all. I looked at her perfectly manicured fingers wrapped around her coffee cup, still tan from weekends at the beach. Even sun kissed, they were so much lighter than my own skin.

"I guess I'm just feeling kind of guilty." The corner of her lip quivered. "I was so young when I had you. The same age you are now." She glanced around the coffee shop and then back at me. "It was okay? Growing up the way you did?"

"It works for us." I lifted a shoulder, wondering why she was bringing this up now. Did she sense I was about to rip apart her world?

"I love you just as much as if I'd raised you myself," she said.

I frowned. "Probably more. Grandma says I'm a pain in the ass."

Anxiety bubbled around in my already troubled belly.

"I have to talk to you about something important," she said just as I opened my mouth to speak.

I shut my trap and rubbed my guitar charm, swallowing the growing lump of dread in my throat. Had she found out? I closed my eyes for a second, bracing myself for a tough conversation.

"I'm pregnant," she said.

I opened my eyes. "What?"

She giggled. "Pregnant."

Glass tinkled in the background. A shout of laughter erupted from the group of girls at the joined tables. I blinked, thrown completely off guard.

"What do you mean?" I wished I could be teleported to an alternate universe where none of this was happening.

"I think you know what I mean." Her smile wobbled. "You okay? You look like you've seen a ghost."

Pregnant? I coughed. This made things worse. Much, much worse. She frowned. Waiting for me to say something. Anything.

"No. It's…um, you don't look pregnant," I managed.

She wiggled in her chair. "Actually I do." She stood up and turned sideways, thrusting out her belly and placing her hand on it. Two older men at the table beside us studied her belly too. It did stick out. A small bulge where months before it had been perfectly flat in a bikini.

I shot death rays at the men, who quickly looked away.

She sat down. "I'm almost five months already. Look at me. I should have known, but I'm so irregular. And my sex drive is fine."

She smiled apologetically as my cheeks reddened and I glanced at the table beside us, knowing the men could hear.

"Sorry," she said. "Too much info, right?"

"Way too much." Images flashed in my head. "Simon's sex drive seems fine too," I mumbled.

"What?" Her smile vanished, and I saw how her lipstick was bleeding over her top lip. She didn't look so perfect anymore.

I thought about shoving my fist down my throat. "I'm just shocked. You know?" My attempt at a laugh rang feeble and insincere. "You're kind of old to be pregnant." It sounded mean even to my ears, but I couldn't take it back. There was so much that couldn't be taken back.

She forced a smile. "I'm not that old. And hey, you'll be a big sister. It'll be fun."

"Yeah. Fun." I choked on a bitter laugh. "At least the baby will be half black. People might believe I'm actually related to someone in the family now."

I glanced around the café, wishing someone would come and interrupt us, wishing Jackson would accidentally start a fire behind the counter, anything to get me away from this conversation with my mom. When my gaze returned to her face, I winced at the need in her eyes. As if she wanted my approval. Needed it. "When did you find out?" I asked, my voice weak and crackling as I tried to sound like I was happy for her.

"Yesterday. At my physical. When I couldn't remember when I'd had my last period, my doctor insisted on a test. Voilà! Pregnant."

"How's Simon taking it?" I asked, chewing on my lip. I already had a pretty good idea.

Mom played with her hair, a hint of a giggle back on her lips. "I think it kind of freaked him out. That's what I get for dating a younger man." She lifted her shoulder and took a quick sip of her decaf and then put the mug down.

"He went out last night with his brother. To celebrate." She made air quote marks with her fingers. "He was hung over and snoring in bed when I went to work this morning." She looked down, tracing a finger along the rim of her mug. "He hasn't gotten drunk in a long time. I guess he just needed to deal with the news."

"I guess he did." My voice cracked again at the end of the sentence.

She glanced up. "It's no big deal. He's not usually a big drinker."

Which was a good thing, apparently.

She folded a hand across her belly, oblivious to the thoughts bouncing around in my head.

"Anyhow, he'll be a great dad. I know he will. Once he's used to the idea. He likes kids. "

Yeah. I've seen that too.

She crossed her legs and leaned back, and I noticed the men watching her with matching expressions of disappointment and openly eavesdropping on our conversation now.

"I'm already past the worst part of pregnancy, and I didn't even know it. How funny is that?"

"Hilarious. Hey, I know. Maybe I'll get pregnant too. You could be a pregnant grandma. Now that would be funny."

"Jaz." She uncrossed her leg and then glared at the men, not as unaware of them as she'd pretended to be. They quickly concentrated on their coffee.

"I thought you'd be a little happier, you know? You and Simon are friends. He'll be like a stepdad now."

A wave of nausea gnawed at my stomach. "He's not my stepdad." I pushed myself away from the table. I couldn't be the one to ruin everything for her. Not now. But I also couldn't make it through another minute with her.

"Listen. I meant to tell you right away that I have an English project to finish. I forgot about it, but it's pretty important and I have to get it done this weekend. Can we go shopping another day?" I stood up.

"Really?" She blinked quickly. "I mean, sure. I was hoping you'd help me pick out some maternity clothes, but yeah, I guess we can do it another time."

"I really do have to go," I said, feeling worse.

"You sure you're okay?" she asked. "You're not upset about me and Simon?"

"I'm fine. Just, you know, swamped with work." My toe tapped up and down, wanting to run.

"You like Simon, right?" Her eyes widened. Her bottom lip quivered a tiny bit. "I thought you'd be excited about a baby."

"I'll see you soon." Instead of answering, I turned from the table and bolted.

The truth was that I had liked her boyfriend. Cougar Bait I called him as a joke because of his age. Too young to be my dad. He was one of the few black people I knew, and we'd gotten along great.

Until last night.

Because last night at Marnie O'Reilly's party, my life had suddenly morphed into a bad imitation of *The Jerry Springer Show.*

It was Simon. Simon with his tongue down the throat of Lacey Stevens. My mom's boyfriend with my best friend. And how could I possibly tell my mom that now?

chapter two

My back pressed against the brick wall of the school as I huddled over my guitar, blocking out the rest of the world and lost in the lyrics to a new song. My cell rang, interrupting my thoughts, and my stomach swooped like a seagull diving for a fish.

Oh, God, please don't let it be Lacey.

Of course, chances weren't great since hardly anyone called instead of texting. Even Grandma texted. But for some reason, Lacey hated it.

I put down my guitar and scooted across the cool grass. Reaching inside my backpack, I grabbed the phone and checked call display. Just as I'd suspected. Lacey. I switched the ringer off and tossed the phone back in my bag.

"Jaz."

I lifted my hand to shield out the sun and peered into the shredded knees on a pair of jeans. "Hey, Ashley. Nice tips." Ashley's short blond hair had pink ends today. She rotated the color of her hair tips in a random pattern. Pink, green, blue. She said the colors had to do with her moods, but I hadn't figured out which color meant what frame of mind.

"Not all of us have your awesome spiral curls. I do what I can with what I've got," Ashley said in her high-pitched voice. When we first met, she'd confessed to hating that she sounded like Minnie Mouse. Her observation made me laugh, but I didn't admit it was kind of true because it obviously bugged her. After she'd told me that, I'd suspected we'd be friends.

"So I thought we were going to meet in the Cave to study before class." Her voice dipped a little lower, the way it did when she wasn't happy. The Cave was an old teachers' lounge converted into a study hall for students. In theory, teachers patrolled it, but mostly they left us alone in there as long as nothing illegal or too noisy went on.

"Oh, shoot. I forgot. I'm so sorry." I dropped my gaze to the grass. I'd totally blanked out on our study date. Stupid of me, especially since our friendship was still pretty new and I didn't want to lose her, the only person my age I wanted to hang out with. She'd just transferred to Westwind for senior year.

"You forgot about studying?" Ashley held out her slim hand to help me up. "Miss 'I like to study more than a normal person my age should ever want to'? Is everything all right?"

"I guess." I grabbed her hand and pulled, and she stumbled since she's shorter than me.

We both laughed as she got her balance. I put my guitar in its case and then bent to pick up my backpack and slung it over my shoulder. "I've got a lot on my mind. I really am sorry."

Ashley tilted her chin, watching me. "Do you want to talk about it?"

"Not really."

Ashley turned toward the front doors. "Okay." Her body language said "slighted," but I couldn't do anything about it.

"So you've probably been up since six to swim this morning?" I said to change the subject.

"Quarter to five. We swam at five-thirty."

I groaned but admired her discipline. Ashley swam competitively at the pool next to her old high school, and though she didn't talk about how good she was, I'd checked her out online and found she held a bunch of records. When I'd asked her about it, she'd shrugged. She'd been much more reactive when I told her I hated to swim. It wasn't entirely true. I just never really got over the time I almost drowned in fourth grade.

"You want to come to the pool after school? I have a lane to myself for two hours. I could spend some time teaching you the front crawl. I have extra suits." She'd become determined to get me in the water, positive she could teach me to swim.

"I have to work tonight."

"Well, another night then. I'm not giving up. No one should be afraid of the water. You have a natural swimmer's build. I bet you'd be really good once you got going."

"Always optimistic, aren't you, Ashley?"

"I can't believe you don't swim," she mumbled.

I shrugged, but in my head I pictured the kids surrounding me in the YMCA pool when I'd been eleven. Swimming around me, blocking me from reaching the ledge, laughing while I panicked and forgot what I'd learned about staying afloat in water and dog-paddled in circles. Terror banged in my chest as I'd struggled to breathe. My head started bobbing up and down while I heard distant gleeful shouts that my color was rubbing off and making the water dirty. I'd thrashed around, trying to keep my head above the water. The faces of my classmates flashed in and out in front of me, laughing and screeching as I struggled.

And then, the surreal panic fled and turned into an absolute certainty that I was going to die. The realization had calmed me, and I'd stopped fighting against the pull of the water taking me under. My lungs stopped burning, and an exquisite sensation of peace took over. I could remember the tangible feeling even now. Six years later. Death welcoming me.

"I can't even float properly," I said to Ashley, trying to push away the memory.

She pffted at me. "When's the last time you tried?"

I shrugged. I vividly remembered the shame. When I didn't come back up, the lifeguard must have finally noticed it wasn't just fun and games in the circle of kids. Maybe their screams changed to panic. I didn't remember him jumping in to rescue me or giving me mouth-to-mouth or anything else until I started breathing again and threw up all over myself.

I'd never gone swimming again after that day. At first I'd been certain that if I put myself in water again, I would die. Or that my color really would rub off and dirty everyone. As I got older that faded, but somehow even the thought of slipping on a bathing suit panicked me. Standing there so exposed.

"You just haven't been taught properly. I'm a good teacher," Ashley said.

She probably was. But I wasn't interested.

The whole fourth grade had been in on it. The ones who didn't actually block me in the water had turned their heads. The teachers and parent volunteers had missed it. Afterward, not one of the kids ever said a thing about their part in my "accident."

After that day, everyone sort of stopped paying attention to me. I learned to take a book outside until we outgrew recess. I never knew if they stopped caring about me because they felt guilty they'd almost killed me, or if they were actually disappointed I hadn't drowned.

"I will get you swimming," Ashley said.

"You can always dream," I said lightly.

Ashley and I stopped then to avoid being plowed over by a group of rowdy boys. They bumped past us yet managed to completely ignore us as if we weren't even there.

"So. I didn't see you at Marnie's party over the weekend. I thought you'd be there," she said after the boys went past.

We went to my locker, and Ashley leaned against the wall while I dialed in my combination.

"I actually was there for a while," I told her as I reached for my English books from the top shelf of my locker. "I took off early." Gently I stood my guitar at the back of the locker.

"Fight with your boyfriend?" She grinned.

"Nathan is not my boyfriend." I scrunched my nose as if something smelled bad, shoved my backpack onto the top shelf, and slammed the door shut.

Ashley licked her lips. They were always chapped from the pool. "Maybe not, but he likes you."

"He likes anything that moves."

"Well, except me. He's not into lesbians." She laughed.

"I'm sure he would be, given the opportunity."

Ashley laughed again. "True."

Nathan was Lacey's roommate and a regular at Marnie's parties, which is where I'd met Ashley the summer before senior year. She had lost an old pocket watch she always carried around in her back pocket and was wandering around upset. When I asked her why, she'd fought off tears and I'd helped her search for the watch. We eventually found it under the cushion of a couch and then bonded over warm, alcohol-free Cokes in the living room, surrounded by a bunch of surprisingly mellow drunks.

Ashley didn't drink because she swam every day except Sunday and didn't want to deal with hangovers or a pissed-off coach. I didn't drink because losing control made me crazy, so we were the always the youngest and straightest people at Marnie's parties, which weren't exactly meant for the high-school crowd.

Ashley used to hang out a lot with an older girl who I'd assumed was her girlfriend, but the other girl had been off in the kitchen smoking dope or something the night Ashley lost the watch, and after that they didn't hang out anymore. I figured they'd broken up, but Ashley didn't talk much about her love life. That was okay, because I didn't talk about mine. Easier, perhaps, since I didn't have one.

Ashley and I headed down the hallway crowded with kids rushing to class.

Everyone at Westwind knew Ashley was gay and that she'd

transferred over from the other high school in town because she'd had enough of bullying. I think most of the Westwind student body wanted to seem cooler, so no one bothered her. We couldn't beat their football team but we could tolerate the first lesbian in Tadita high-school history. The first open one anyhow. Go Westwind.

Mostly everyone treated her the same way they treated me. They ignored her. This late in the game, that didn't seem to bother Ashley.

"Lacey was really out of it at the party," she said after a moment.

"What else is new?"

Ashley glanced sideways at me but didn't comment. Lacey had never made an effort to get along with her, but Ashley wasn't the type to trash talk.

"You'll never guess who did show up," Ashley said as we maneuvered our way around bodies going the opposite direction.

I didn't guess.

"Your mom's boyfriend, Simon."

"No kidding?" I kept my voice level, my eyes straight ahead.

"He came by to pick up his younger brother. Simon was the one who ended up getting wasted, though, and Damien ended up driving him home."

Before she said anything else, I cut her off. "What an idiot. It's like he's trying to recapture his youth or something."

"Simon's not that much older than Marnie. He's younger than your mom, right?"

"I have no idea how old Marnie is," I said as we slipped inside our English class. We slid into chairs in the relative safety of the middle row just as the bell rang.

"Twenty-two," Ashley supplied.

I peeked at the back of the room where Jackson usually sat. He raised an eyebrow and tilted his head.

"Hey," he mouthed.

I couldn't help a slight smile but forced myself to turn away, ignoring the little solo jig my stomach performed. So, we were going to acknowledge each other now? With an effort I forced myself not to look back again. I failed, and when I peeked, he was smiling. I dropped my gaze to my desk, my cheeks blazing.

At the front of the class, Mr. Dustan began giving instructions. His favorite student came around and dropped exams on our desks. When I finished the test, I looked back at Jackson. As if he felt my eyes on him, he glanced up and raised his pencil in the air, saluting me. A smile turned up my lips, but I got up and took my paper to the front of the class and left.

Alone.

• • •

When I walked into the living room, Simon was sprawled on Grandma's comfy leather couch. He made me sick, so I focused on Grandma and ignored him.

Not a strand of her storm-cloud-colored hair was out of place. She looked a little frail in her old-lady jeans and yellow cardigan, but under it was one tough woman. The only time I'd ever seen her cry was after Grandpa Joe died. And that was only once. Never since.

On the couch opposite Simon, Mom looked relaxed, but obviously appearances could be deceptive. I'd bet money she'd only included me in her meeting with Grandma to be a buffer, in case Grandma disapproved of her pregnancy. Grandma would play it down in front of me. To her, I was still a child.

"Hey, Jaz, my second favorite lady. How's your song writing going?" Simon sounded on the verge of revealing the punch line to a secret joke.

"Second?" Grandma asked. "What about me?"

He threw back his head and laughed. "It's a tie." He held up his hands in defense.

I rolled my eyes. "Can you get on with this? I have to go to work." Their news was not something I wanted to hear over and over again. I'd rather go back in time and erase everything. Maybe I'd start with Simon's existence. He frowned at me but I paid no attention, fighting to keep in my anger and the desire to stand up and tell everyone what I'd seen. The low-down dirty dog.

My stomach grumbled and I glanced at the coffee table. As always, Grandma had snacks laid out on her expensive china. She didn't like fancy things going to waste and used the china at every opportunity. She had the same metabolism as me and believed in eating carbs. I grabbed a homemade cinnamon bun off a plate and shoved a chunk in my mouth as I plunked myself in the La-Z-Boy chair off to the side of the couches.

Simon stared at me, tugging on his earlobe. "How's it going, Jaz?" he asked, tilting his head. "Everything all right?"

I pointed to my full mouth, chewing slowly. He'd have to get used to silence and snarky answers. Our friendship was so over.

"She's at the top of her class with most of her grades," Grandma bragged. "And still a musical genius. Always on her guitar and writing new songs."

I shoved more cinnamon bun in my mouth and kept chewing. I could add I was still pretty much socially inept to even things out.

"Beauty and brains," Mom said, smiling at me a little too hard.

"Good thing she takes after her grandma," Grandma said.

Mom snorted. "Well. On that fitting note. We have a surprise for you." Mom leaned forward and picked her purse up off the floor. She unzipped it and pulled out a small, blue velvet box and thrust it into Grandma's hand.

Simon leaned forward, watching them with his huge paw-like hand reaching up to cover his mouth. His lips were turned up in a smile, and I wanted to snatch it off his face. What right did he have to look excited?

"What's this?" Grandma asked, glancing at Simon and then back at my mom.

Mom leaned back against the couch. "Open it."

I shoved more cinnamon bun in my mouth.

Grandma squealed when she looked inside the box. "This isn't jewelry." She pulled out a pregnancy test with a bright blue positive sign in the square in the middle.

I stuck my tongue out, disgusted. "Gross. She peed on that thing."

Grandma chuckled. "I'm going to be a grandma!" She squealed and wrapped her arms around Mom. For the first time in years I witnessed them hugging. Grandma broke away and turned to me, her eyes moist with tears. "Did you know about this? I can't believe you kept a secret! You're terrible at secrets."

"I am not." I glared at Simon, but he was grinning so I looked back at Grandma.

Grandma put the pregnancy test back in the box and brought it to her chest. "You'll be a big sister." She was cuddling the pee stick.

"Lucky me." I looked down and noticed a tiny hole in the big toe of my sock.

"Jaz." I glanced up. Grandma's eyebrows were knit together tight. "That was rude." She turned to Simon. "So when is the big day?"

"Hello? We're not getting married," Mom said.

"I meant the due date," Grandma said and swatted at her knee. "When have you ever done things in the right order?"

Mom laughed, and the three of them all started talking at the same time.

"Hey Jaz, the baby's due two days after my twenty-eighth birthday. How cool a present is that?" Simon called to me. "I phoned my dad with the news, and he's flying across the pond a few months after the baby's born."

As if I should still care. Simon's dad moved to England years ago when he split with Simon's mom. I knew Simon would be pumped about seeing him again, but I hardened my heart, trying not to think about our long talks about absent fathers. I didn't want to care about Simon or his life anymore.

I imagined myself standing up and pointing an accusing finger at Simon. Not cool at all, you two-timing freak. How far did you go after I saw you making out with Lacey? Did you get her pregnant too?

I pictured Grandma smashing her good china on Simon's head. I swallowed the permanent wedge in my throat and added an image of my mom collapsing on the floor in a ladylike faint to my fantasy. But then I imagined her grabbing her stomach. Losing the baby.

"Jasmine?" Grandma said.

I glanced up.

"This is great news, isn't it?" Grandma spoke in a soft voice that told me she suspected something.

"Clearly much happier than it was seventeen years ago when she made the same announcement," I said and stood, almost knocking the plate of cinnamon buns off the table with my knee. "I have to get going." If I stayed another moment, I'd burst into tears. Or spill the secret. And I didn't want to do either.

"Jasmine," Mom and Grandma said at the same time with equal unhappiness in their voices. I had the urge to yell, "Jinx. You owe me a beer," at them.

"Where do you have to go right now?" The wrinkles on Grandma's face deepened as she stared up at me. "This is a celebration."

I started coughing and couldn't stop.

When I got myself under control, I saw a look pass between Simon and Mom as if they felt sorry for me. As if I was acting like a jerk because I was jealous of their baby or something. As if I was the one doing something wrong.

"I have to work." True. Even if it wasn't for an hour.

I ran from the living room and raced upstairs to change into my work stuff and grab my guitar. I hurried back down with my guitar case slung over my shoulder.

"Can I use Grandpa's car to go to work?" I called to Grandma in the living room. I didn't drive it often because I was afraid of getting in an accident and ruining our only connection to him. Funny that Grandpa had been gone so long, but it was still his car. It always would be. It even had the faint smell of him lingering in the cloth seats.

"Why're you taking your guitar to work?" Grandma yelled.

"I'll be jamming after work. At Lacey's," I lied. That was the last place I'd go, but I'd find somewhere to play.

"Fine. Drive carefully."

I went to the front door to grab the key off the hook where Grandma kept it.

"She's the one acting like a baby," I heard Grandma say as the door banged behind me. "But she'll get used to the idea. It'll grow on her."

I had the urge to sit down on the front lawn and cry. Simon had gotten drunk and made out with my best friend while my pregnant mom waited at home.

But I was the one who got to be the bad guy. And keep his secret.

chapter three

I rushed through the parking lot of Grinds, wiping my clammy hands on my pants. I only had two minutes to spare before my shift started. I'd gone for a long drive to try to clear my messed-up thoughts. Hurrying inside, I slipped through the employee entrance and clocked in.

A long line of impatient customers swirled around the café. Lacey looked up from the cash register, her eyes staring right into mine, before turning back to a woman in line. I blew out a breath of relief that she was too busy to talk, pulled my blue apron off a hook, and joined Amber in the Pit. I didn't deal with customers most shifts. Amber knew that wasn't my forte.

"Thank goodness you're here. It's crazy." Amber squirted caramel in a decorative flower pattern on top of a mug of foam. "Some convention across the street. They all want their coffee yesterday."

Lacey called out coffee orders while Amber and I slipped into a busy but comfortable groove. The rush lasted for almost an hour. As soon as it ended, Amber said she was heading into the office to do paperwork.

"How come you hired Jackson Morgan?" I asked as Amber pulled off her apron and smoothed out her whiskey-colored hair.

I kind of hoped she'd tell me more about him. How he ended up working at Grinds. What his favorite color was. If he was into girls like me.

"You have a problem with him?" She folded her apron into a square.

My cheeks burned. "No, of course not. He just doesn't seem, I don't know, like the coffee-shop type." I rubbed at my guitar charm and glanced out into the café.

"There is no type, honey. Do you know how hard it is to get part-time workers these days? Unless he's not doing his job or he's stealing from me, he's more than welcome to work here. He's a good kid."

"That's probably not what his parole officer says," I mumbled, and my cheeks flamed again. By trying to hide my interest, I sounded like a jerk.

"Hey." Amber smacked my arm lightly. "You of all people don't strike me as the judgmental type." She gave me a dirty look before slipping out of the work area and heading for her office at the back of the shop.

I made a face at her back but avoided looking toward the cash register, where I felt Lacey's presence in the pit of my stomach. I kept busy fetching milk from the cooler, filling steel carafes, topping up mixes, and cleaning up spills.

Inevitably Lacey sauntered over to the Pit and stood still, just staring at me. I ignored her.

"So, how's it going?" she finally asked.

"Fine." I wished there was a mute button I could press to keep her from saying more.

"You going to stay mad at me forever?" she asked.

I scrubbed the counter like I was sanding Grandma's old furniture. From the corner of my eye, I saw Lacey jut her hip out. She blew a bubble with her gum and breathed out until it popped.

"I'm sorry. I mean…about what happened," she said. "We were both really drunk."

I scrubbed harder, concentrating on the counter and not making eye contact with her. "You weren't too drunk to know it was Simon."

She shifted from one foot to another. "I know. I'm sorry. I don't know how it happened."

I willed her not to say anything more. The less I knew, the better.

"This is really awkward," she said.

"You could say that." A surge of anger hit me, and I glanced straight at her. "How could you do that? Simon, Lacey. It was Simon."

"I was drunk, Jaz. It was stupid."

"Drunk is always your excuse."

Lacey didn't speak for a moment. "Ouch," she finally said and lifted a hand and studied her nails. "I didn't mean to get that drunk. I feel terrible."

I sighed. Didn't she get it? Simon was almost family. Last year when some kid at the mall called me an Oreo, it was Simon I went to. He was the only person I could talk to about things like that.

"You're a strong, beautiful girl with talent and smarts," Simon had said when I told him. "Not a cookie." He'd rubbed the top of my head. "No one can take away who you are inside or out. Don't let other people make you feel bad about who you are."

I'd dropped my head. "I look black on the outside. But I'm not."

"You are black," Simon said, standing straighter. "And that's something to be proud of."

I couldn't look at Simon. I didn't feel like I shared or deserved that heritage. That pride in being black. I wasn't the real thing, one way or the other.

Simon had moved closer and put a finger under my chin, forcing me to look at him. "Our people fought for equality and respect for hundreds of years. You're up for this. You don't have to earn it, Jaz."

But I wasn't sure. Not then or now.

"Jazzy?" Lacey said.

I glared at her. After standing up for me, after being part of my family for so long, Simon had ruined it. Lacey had ruined it with him.

Lacey must have read my expression because her eyes filled with tears. She rubbed them, smudging her black eyeliner.

"You know how I get. It didn't mean anything. You know that, right? Can you forgive me? Please?"

I glanced away, not able to stand the sight of her. I did know how she got. How many times had I told her she shouldn't get trashed and make out with random dudes? How often had I stood by her while she dealt with the morning-after remorse?

"We're talking about my mom's boyfriend. It's not like you got a stain on my favorite shirt or something. I can't just make it go away."

"I know. I really hate myself, if that makes you feel better." She chewed a fake fingernail and then wiped under her eyes, smearing her makeup even more. "How can I make you forgive me?"

That was my cue to tell her that it was okay. That she shouldn't drink so much. Give her a pep talk. "There's not a lot you can do."

She sucked in a quick breath and sniffled. "I can't lose you over this, Jaz. You're the only person who accepts me for who I am."

I stood straighter; I wouldn't let her talk her way out. Not from this. "Does Simon know I saw you?"

Lacey's hair flitted back and forth over her shoulder as she shook her head. "I don't think so. I didn't say anything about it."

"And you swear there's nothing going on between you two now?" I didn't ask how far it had gone. I didn't want to know. Even though I did.

"Of course not. I swear. I promise. Nothing."

I turned from her and went back to scrubbing the counter.

"Don't hate me, okay?" she begged.

But at that minute, I did. Hatred filled me. There was blackness in my heart for my messed-up best friend who, even with her crooked lipstick and smeared eyes, managed to look vulnerable and sad instead of cheap and slutty.

Lacey grabbed my hand as I continued my psycho scrubbing. "You're not going to tell your mom, are you? She'd totally hate me, and I really love your mom."

"You have a really messed-up way of showing people you love them." I crossed my arms and glanced over to the cash register as two customers bustled up to the order area chatting about caffeine cravings.

Lacey patted my arm. Her mouth turned up in a lopsided smile. "Don't write a song about it either, okay?"

I watched her walk away to take orders and wondered how she was going to react to the news that my mom was pregnant with

Simon's baby. I hoped it made her feel much, much worse about what she'd done. I wanted her to bleed a little inside.

The customers ordered plain coffee, so Lacey strolled back to my work area. She leaned against the sink, watching me pour coffee into Grinds mugs.

I put the drinks on the counter, and when I turned back, Lacey pirouetted for me. "Do you like my new work shirt?" The white shirt dipped so low that the lace of her frilly bra showed.

Was she kidding? Her expression drooped when I didn't give her a compliment. Did she think all was forgiven that easily?

I glanced at the clock on the wall. "Look, my shift is over. I gotta go." I turned.

"Call me soon, okay?" she said.

I didn't answer her as I headed for the time clock. Lacey was my best friend, but my mom was my mom. Even if our relationship wasn't exactly conventional.

I had to make sure it never happened again.

"Lacey?" I called as she made her way back to the cash area. She glanced back at me.

"My mom's pregnant," I said in a flat voice. "Simon's going to be a father."

We looked each other straight in the eyes. "Don't ever tell anyone what happened, okay?"

Lacey's eyes opened wider, and her face seemed to get paler. "Oh. God. I'm so sorry." Her hand went up to cover her mouth.

I shook my head, not wanting to hear more. "Just don't say anything, okay?"

"Not a soul." Lacey made an X across her chest and closed her eyes and took a deep breath. "She'll never ever know."

• • •

My calloused left fingers pressed the spaces between the frets on my guitar, and I strummed the wire strings with the other hand. Strumming is the true act of playing guitar. The hardened tips of my fingers felt soothed. The itchy cravings I had when I wasn't playing were gone. I softly sang the words to Neil Diamond's "I Am…I Said."

In my mind, I remembered Grandpa accompanying me with his beautiful aching voice. He'd taught me the song as a duet to be ironic, he said. His sense of humor drove Grandma crazy. A tear formed in the corner of my eye, and I let it plop down my cheek without stopping to wipe it away.

Someone cleared his throat.

Embarrassed, I dropped my fingers from the strings and looked up. I'd almost forgotten I wasn't alone in the privacy of my room. Not wanting to go home after my shift, I'd walked to the park behind Grinds and propped myself up on top of a picnic bench. This time of the year, the park was abandoned, so I'd laid my guitar case out beside me and gotten lost in my own music.

Jackson took a step forward and, with a serious expression, reached into his back pocket and threw a bill inside my case. It was a twenty.

A tiny smile replaced the ache in my heart. "I'm not busking," I told him. "I don't want money."

"I honestly felt like I should pay for that. You're really good."

I was trying to think of a response when his cell started ringing from his jacket pocket. He lifted his finger to tell me to hang on and then started digging around. "Just a sec."

He pulled out his phone.

"Hello?" he said. He paused and turned away from me. "Yeah. I already told you. I'll get you your stuff."

I stared at his back, noticing the nice round shape of his butt in his jeans, but I shook my head. Was he doing a drug deal right in front of me? I didn't know whether to laugh or get up and stomp away. I decided it wasn't my business and tried not to eavesdrop on the rest of the conversation. A gust of wind had started to chill me, so I tucked my hands under my butt to warm my fingers.

"Sorry," he said after he'd hung up. "Unpleasant business."

I shrugged, trying to pretend I didn't know what he was up to. I pulled my guitar strap over my head and off my shoulder, then reached inside my guitar case and took out his twenty.

"I wish I could sing like you," he said.

I held out the money to him. "I'm not that good."

He pulled his hands back to avoid the bill. "Uh. Yeah, you are."

"I'm not taking your money." I frowned. "Seriously."

"I like to support the arts," he said.

I tried to shove the money at him, but he backed away, laughing.

"I'm not the arts. I play for me. I don't want money for my music." I waved the money at him, wanting to get it out of my hand.

"Everyone wants money. It's called dough because we all 'knead' it." He wiggled his eyebrows up and down.

I frowned at the cash in my fingers, holding it like it was tainting my fingers. "Are you making fun of me?"

"Whoa. Definitely not fun making. If it fouls your mood that much, give me the money back. I just wanted you to know I admired your skills." He held out his hand.

I thrust the twenty inside his hand. "I don't want your money."

"All the better for me. I like free stuff," he said cheerfully. He folded the twenty and tucked it in his back pocket.

"Hey, what's the difference between a guitar and a fish?" he asked.

My eyebrows pressed together with my frown.

"You can tune a guitar but you can't tuna fish." He grinned, and his smile was so ridiculous but infectious that the tight ball inside me relaxed a little. "Come on, Jaz. Don't tell me I can't even make you smile at a joke that bad. "

I shook my head and stared at him for a minute, trying to figure him out. He stared back. "You're not like other boys in Tadita," I told him. The wind gusted again and whipped his hair around. I zipped my jacket all the way up under my chin, wishing I'd brought a scarf.

"And for that observation, I'm sure they would thank you," he said.

I smiled, and he pointed at my mouth and grinned. "Look! You smiled."

"I'm sorry," I said.

"About what?"

"For being a B. I know you were just fooling around. It's not you. It's just that I've had kind of a bad day." I turned to my guitar and lifted it, placing it gently back in its case and closing the case.

"You want to talk about it?"

"Not really."

He laughed. "Don't hold back. Tell me how you really feel."

I slid off the picnic table and picked up my guitar case. I wished I could tell him. Well, maybe not him. But someone.

"Hey," he said softly. "You okay?"

I shook my head and started walking, not wanting to bawl like a big baby or something in front of him.

"Jaz," he called and walked toward me, catching up quickly with his longer legs. "I seem to keep saying the wrong thing. I just came over to see if you're working tonight."

I remembered how he was new in town and probably didn't have a lot of people to talk to. Outside of drug deals. Sighing, I slowed down a little so I wasn't speed-walking to get away from him. "I just finished a shift."

"Oh. Too bad," he said.

Those simple words made a nice dent in my foul mood.

We walked toward Grinds. "You heading inside?" he asked. "Want to have a coffee before I start work? I'll even let you buy since you don't want to take my money." He grinned.

I thought of Lacey still inside. "Nope. I have homework. I have to go home."

His expression changed and then he shrugged. "Okay. Well, see ya round," he said.

I started walking toward Grandpa's car in the parking lot.

"You're pretty good with that guitar. It's an Alvarez, right?" Jackson called.

I stopped and turned back. "How'd you know that?"

"I know some things. People might surprise you if you look harder. Sometimes you have to look beneath the surface."

I wondered if I even wanted to know what he meant and decided, no, I didn't.

chapter four

The holidays came and went. I managed to avoid my mom and dodge her calls until she caught me off guard by calling my cell from an unlisted number. I'd just finished a shift at Grinds, and when I answered and heard her voice, I swiveled on my chair away from Lacey. She'd parked herself at my table and was across from me, sipping coffee and flipping through a celebrity magazine.

I zoned out as Mom went on and on about me not returning her calls. She kept talking, but I didn't pay attention until I heard her calling my name.

"Jaz? Jaz? Are you listening?"

I refocused on her voice. "Sorry, what did you say?"

"I said Simon wants to take us out for supper tomorrow night. Do you think you could possibly make it this time?" Even over the phone her crankiness was tangible. Pregnancy seemed to be catching up with her fast. "You haven't seen him since Christmas."

"Uh. Sorry. I already have plans." I chewed my fingernail and swirled back to face the table but kept my eyes off Lacey.

Mom blew out a big breath of air. "Okay," she finally said, her voice strained as if she was trying really hard not to freak out on me. "So when? What's your work schedule like this week?"

"Busy, very busy." I said, and glanced up. Lacey was pretending not to eavesdrop as she licked her finger and flipped a magazine page.

"Come on, Jasmine. You've ignored Simon since you found out we're pregnant. He's tried giving you space, but he thinks you're still mad at him. He's going to be the father of your brother or sister and your stepfather, so deal with it." She sighed loudly.

I chewed my lip. "He's not my stepfather unless there was a wedding I didn't hear about."

"Well, he might be someday. Jaz, what's the matter? You and Simon used to get along great. What's going on? Is it the baby?"

"No. It's nothing. I'm just super busy. Actually, I'm working on homework right now, so I should really go." I wanted to hang up. Forget Mom and her stupid baby. Forget her stupid boyfriend and the kiss I couldn't wipe out of my memory no matter how hard I tried.

Lacey looked up and raised her eyebrows, but I ignored her.

"We need to work this out," my mom said.

"There's nothing to work out."

"What's wrong with you?" she snapped impatiently, definitely not sounding like her usual self.

"Nothin'. I'll talk to you later." I pressed End.

"Whatever," I said, even though the phone had no dial tone. I shut it and threw it on the table.

Lacey smirked at me. "Homework?" she asked. "I didn't know you lied."

"You want me to tell her the truth about why I'm avoiding Simon?" I asked.

Lacey looked down at her magazine, pretending she wasn't the reason for my new case of *liar, liar, pants on fire*. My leg bounced up and down under the table, and I fought the urge to get up and bolt.

Hands slid over my eyes then, blocking my sight. "Hey, sexy," a deep burly voice growled in my ear, tickling my earlobe. "Want to run away with me?"

"Hey, Nathan." His voice was his most distinctive quality, rich and powerful, like a radio disc jockey's.

Nathan and Lacey were two misfits who'd been friends in high school. For once I was glad he constantly orbited around Lacey and always flirted with me. Usually it made me uncomfortable, but right then he was a welcome distraction.

I pulled his hands off my eyes, turned to him, and smiled. He grinned down at me, looking a little surprised by the friendly welcome, but he gave me his trademark two-fingered "hang loose" sign. Bracelets dangled from his dark wrists, and gold chains twirled in layers around his neck. He had giant, fake diamond earrings in both ears. Bargain-basement bling. Nathan's impression of big-city black. He'd visited New York a while back and returned to Tadita using gangsta slang.

Most people around here just ignored him or stared at him like he was from another planet. Eventually he toned it down. Once when he'd been drunk, he'd told me that his cousin in New York accused him of acting white. I guess that's what brought on the change. "I ain't white," he'd told me as if it was a bad thing. How was that supposed to make me feel? Had he looked at my mom lately?

"How'd you know it was me?" Nathan turned his chair backward and straddled it.

"Besides the fact that you reek like a forest fire from all your chain-smoking?" Lacey threw down her magazine. She made a face at him, but it was an old argument.

The tiny old house that the two of them rented was messy and smelled like smoke, but despite her complaining, neither of them seemed to care. They'd moved in after high school, both needing to get away from home for different reasons: Lacey because stepfather number two developed an intense interest in her well-being, and Nathan because his stepfather used him as a punching bag.

Nathan discovered that his thrill for heights could make him serious money in the construction business and had found a house he could afford to live in. Lacey followed, and he let her pay a third of the rent instead of half.

"Your hands feel like sandpaper," I said, thankful for the interruption. "And how could I mistake that voice? Anyhow, I'm smarter than I look."

"You look smart enough to run away with me." He grinned. "Nothing stopping you."

"Except about four years." Lacey leaned across the table to smack his head. "She's jailbait. Leave her alone."

"Jaz is wise beyond her years," Nathan said, running a hand across his shaved head.

"Too wise to fall for your crap," Lacey said.

I ignored the insults flying back and forth and sneaked a peek behind the coffee counter. In the Pit, Jackson was whipping up a special coffee for a regular customer. He smiled a half grin and tugged at his earring. He truly rocked the apron with a complete lack of effort. I lifted my fingers to wave at him and then blushed harder.

He wasn't even looking at me. He was beaming at a skinny blond girl approaching the counter. I tucked my hand in my lap and dropped my glance to the table. What did I expect? He'd wave and then leap across the counter and ask me out?

So what if he was nice to me? So what if my insides fluttered when he flirted with me? Which he did on a regular basis. Was I actually crushing on him? As far as I could tell Jackson flirted with every girl who came within ten feet of him. I thought about Grandpa. He would definitely not have approved of a drug dealer. But then I remembered my vow not to listen to the rumors about Jackson and frowned.

"I want to go to a party," I announced, interrupting Lacey and Nathan, who thankfully had been too busy arguing to see my lame wave at a boy not even looking at me. "Who will buy me some beer?"

They both stopped talking and stared at me as if I'd suddenly sprouted fairy wings.

"What? It's not like I've never been to a party before," I said. The anger in the pit of my stomach wouldn't go away. I intended to drown it.

"No," Lacey said. "But you've never demanded to go to one in that voice before. You sound totally grouchy."

"And you're not usually the beer type, kid," Nathan added.

"More like Dr Pepper," Lacey said.

"Well, things change," I said. "I'm bored. Bored with coffee. Bored with school. Bored with everything."

I didn't add that I was bored with Grandma's nonstop chatter about the new baby. Bored with Lacey talking about herself. Bored with Ashley training for swim meets with no time for me outside school.

Lacey's eyebrows arched. "You sure everything's okay?"

"Fine. I just want to have some fun for once. Is that so wrong?"

"Can't blame a girl for wanting to have fun," Nathan said.

Lacey twirled hair around her finger. "That was your mom on the phone earlier? How's she doing? With Simon and the baby and stuff."

"Who cares?" I didn't meet her eyes. I didn't want to talk about them. Especially not with her.

Nathan grinned. "Marnie's having a bash tonight. We can go there to party."

I pushed back on my chair and jumped to my feet. "Good. Will you buy me some beer?" I pulled a crumpled twenty from the front pocket of my jeans.

Nathan grabbed the money. "I'll buy two cases if that's what you want." He untangled himself from his chair and slung an arm across my shoulder.

"Nathan, she's just a kid," Lacey said.

"Thanks, Nathan." I didn't squirm away from him like I normally did. I glared at Lacey. "I already have a mother, you know. In fact, I have two."

"I'm just sayin'." Lacey held up her hands. "Whatever. It's your hangover."

"Like you said, she's young. Hangovers don't last. Come on." Nathan led me toward the exit.

I glanced back at Jackson. The blond he'd been smiling at had vanished, but he was talking to someone else. I put a little wiggle in my walk. As if I knew what sexy even looked like.

• • •

"Whoa. Slow down a little." Lacey chugged the remains of a beer and squished up beside me on an old brown corduroy couch in Marnie's living room. I leaned over to the cooler in front of us and grabbed another bottle, twisting off the cap and pitching it on the carpet like a normal irresponsible party person. I felt pleasantly dizzy.

I giggled, an unnatural noise. Even my stomach loosened, like I'd relaxed a fist inside. More likely, I'd drowned it. Why hadn't I done this before? Drinking made the party much more interesting. For once I'd become one of the fuzzy, happy ones.

Usually I hung back and observed the older kids crammed into Marnie's small house. Stoners hung in the kitchen and drinkers in the living room, while couples hooked up upstairs. When Ashley was there, she'd hang out with me and we'd talk about music or I'd play guitar, but for some reason she wasn't at this party. Just as well.

"Hey, good looking." Nathan slid onto the couch, pressing his leg suggestively up against mine. He always did that to tease me and I always moved away, but this time I left my leg where it was, feeling the warmth. The connection.

He put his hand on my knee and squeezed. I reached over and squeezed his knee back, giggling.

"Whoa. You are getting hammered," he said.

"Got a problem with that?" I swallowed back a hiccup and grinned.

He slid an arm over my shoulder. "Not even a little if it makes you this friendly."

I leaned against him. Drunk, I relaxed as his fingers massaged my shoulders, working out knots.

A song blared over the speakers in the living room. I couldn't name it if I'd tried, but I was feeling it. Lacey jumped up from beside me and grabbed the hand of some guy standing with his buddy near the couch.

"Dance with me," she demanded and pouted her lips in her practiced sexy way. She wiggled in front of him, shaking her money-makers.

The guy's friend punched him on the shoulder in a congratulatory salute as he pulled Lacey to the makeshift dance floor in the middle of the tiny living room. The two of them immediately started grinding.

Nathan rubbed my neck to the beat of the song and we watched Lacey.

"He is so getting lucky tonight." I leaned against Nathan. "Lacey is such a sure thing."

He laughed his agreement.

I closed one eye to focus on them as they moved to the beat of the song blasting on the stereo. I wondered what it was like. What sex was like.

"I don't blame her this time. That boy is seriously hot," I slurred.

Nathan stopped massaging my neck and leaned toward my ear. "You're not interested in guys like that."

I studied the guy dancing with Lacey. Tight T-shirt. Low riding jeans. Boots. Long blond hair and stocky build. The polar opposite of Simon, thank God.

"No. Tonight I think I am." I hiccuped and giggled, finding myself terribly funny.

"Nah. Stick with your own kind." He buried his face in my neck, tickling me with his breath. "Did I mention I'm deep and intellectual?"

I punched him on his shoulder. "My own kind? I don't have my own kind." I poked my finger into his scrawny chest, brave from the liquor surging through my veins. "And anyhow, who said you're deep and intellectual?"

"I know I am." He blew softly in my ear. "You may not be all black, but you're all beautiful."

"Gee, thanks." I hiccuped again and supported myself against him.

"You're black enough for me," he whispered.

"Not anyone else. And by the way, who said construction workers are intellectual? That's not a job qualification. And the only time you're deep is when you smoke too much dope." I shook my finger at him and took another swig of beer. "Don't you know that's very bad for you?"

"You don't need a degree to be smart," he mumbled.

"Tell my grandma that." I lifted my bottle in a salute and imitated her voice. "Jasmine, the most important thing you will need in the world is a college degree."

He laughed. "Yeah? Well, a brother knocked up your mom when she was sixteen. That didn't require a degree."

"Seventeen. And she got her degree after I was born. Instead of raising me, she let my grandparents do it." I raised my bottle in another toast and took a big swig.

"I guess she kind of sucked at being a mom."

I laughed until beer leaked out of my nose, which made me laugh harder while I mopped it up with my sleeve. "You think?"

"I saw her and Simon the other day. He was rubbing her belly like he'd done something really great."

"Ha! A lot of talent it takes to get my mom pregnant. Not like he's the first." I turned my attention back to Lacey and her dance partner.

Nathan touched my hand. "You pissed? About your mom being pregnant?"

"Why would I care?" I leaned back as the room spun in pleasant circles.

"I don't know. You'll be a sister. Maybe that'll be cool?"

"Nathan. Shut up about my mom and Simon." The conversation detracted from my happy buzz.

He lightly stroked the back of my hand. Nice little jolts rolled over my skin. I lifted my bottle to my lips, watching Nathan. His eyelids looked droopy, almost sexy. When he slowly licked his lips, an unexpected surge rushed through me.

Nathan?

I was drunk. Very drunk.

He reached for me, took the bottle from my hand, and leaned forward in slow motion. I watched his head move toward me. His full lips pried mine open. They were soft and wet. I tasted smoke. I inhaled the smell of beer on his breath.

He pulled away from me, sighing and smiling. "I've wanted to do that for a long, long time."

An alarm rang in my head, but it was fuzzy. How far was this going to go? I didn't say anything. For a minute, I dropped my eyes and enjoyed being wanted.

He leaned down and pressed his cheek against mine. "You okay? I mean, is this okay?"

I didn't answer, which seemed to pass for shyness. He stood and pulled on my hand. "Come on. Let's go somewhere a little more private."

I wondered if Nathan could take away my emptiness. I held his darker hand and allowed myself to be led stumbling toward the stairs, passing couples dancing or making out. Nathan slid an arm around my waist when I tripped. He led me up the stairs into a dark bedroom.

"Jaz," he whispered. His hand touched my hair, and he rubbed it gently between his fingers. He looked almost sinister in the dark. "You're so beautiful."

My eyes slowly adjusted to the blackness. A dresser was covered with clothes and pushed up against the wall. Behind a tiny door to the right was a small bathroom. And in the middle of the room a big bed mocked me.

"Marnie's room," Nathan whispered and licked my neck.

I guessed he'd been there before and I had an urge to laugh at how ridiculous we were acting. Making out and sneaking off to Marnie's messy room in the middle of a drinking party. He kissed me again on the mouth, sticking his tongue in deeper. I tried to feel a little bit of the glow I'd felt earlier. Zilch. Nausea zipped from my stomach to my throat.

I pulled away, my buzz fading. I opened my mouth to tell Nathan I'd never gone past kissing a boy from a different school in eighth grade. A boy who later told me it had been a dare to see if he could get the skinny black girl to kiss him. He'd won twenty bucks, thanks to me.

Nathan shushed me before I could get out a word and pulled me toward the bed in the middle of the room. A cheap floral bedspread covered it, the colors faded and worn. Like me. I wanted to curl up in a little ball inside the covers.

Nathan kissed me again and I resisted, but he didn't seem to notice. He pushed me back so I was sitting on the bed. I tried to squirm away, but he chuckled and bent over, making funny noises in his throat.

"Don't be shy. It's just me." The weight of his body pressed on top of me. His necklaces dangled down against my skin. "You want this. You want it."

Did I? Was this what I wanted?

Claustrophobia strangled me. My stomach lurched with nausea. I pushed my hands against him but he resisted. His ribs poked against my skin. My hip bones ached as he crushed against me.

"No, Nathan. I don't want to," I whispered.

He groaned. "Oh, baby, you do. This is exactly what you want. It's okay. I love you. I love you."

My eyes closed. This was all my fault. I'd gotten myself into this mess with my own stupidity. I held back tears and shame as he struggled to undo my tight jeans.

"No." I reached down to push him away.

"It's okay," he interrupted. "You're beautiful. Let me see you."

He grabbed my wrists and held them back. I shook my head.

"No," I said but it came out weakly, without conviction, and he didn't hear me. No one heard me. God. I was such an idiot. I deserved this. I gritted my teeth, and tears spilled down my cheeks. I was alone. Violated. Exactly what I deserved.

"No," I said louder. "I don't want to." I brought my knee up. Not enough to hurt him but enough to alarm him.

He groaned and moved back. "Hey." He stopped struggling and collapsed on top of me. "What the hell?"

I stared at the ceiling. His full body weight took the breath out of me, and I pushed to get him off. He rolled over and up onto his elbow. His dark skin, even darker in the shadows, made mine look pale, almost white. I stared at it, aching.

"What are you playin' at?" He sat up, rubbing his bald head.

I blinked back fresh tears and bit my lip but didn't answer.

He pushed himself off the bed, shaking his head. "You're a tease." He swore as he zipped up his pants. I didn't even know they'd been undone. "You're lucky, you know. Not everyone would stop after the way you were leading me on."

I swallowed hard to keep bile inside. "Thank you," I said with as much sarcasm as I could muster.

"Shit." He shook his head again and coughed. "I forget how young you are sometimes. Seventeen."

I sat up and hugged my arms around myself.

The corner of his top lip turned upward. He reached for my

hand. "Not many chicks are still innocent at your age. I kind of like it. I guess I can wait for you. For a little while."

I pulled away, pretending to scratch behind my back.

"Don't worry. This wasn't a onetime thing," he said softly. "I'm into you."

I shook my head quickly back and forth. No. It was definitely a onetime thing. Alcohol induced. I wanted no part of doing that again. My head swam from the amount I'd drunk. So much for forgetting my problems. I'd just made them worse.

As I got up, the charms on my bracelet clanged softly against each other. I hoped dead people couldn't see what was happening. Grandpa Joe would have keeled over at my behavior. Well, keeled over again.

"You need a drink?" Nathan asked.

"No," I said quickly. "Go on down. I'll be there in a minute or so." My cheeks flamed, and I willed him to go away.

He leaned over to kiss me, but I turned my head so he kissed my cheek. "I'll meet you downstairs," I repeated.

"Sure. Okay."

He reached for my hand. "We'll finish this."

I flinched. As soon as he closed the door, I ran to the bathroom, barely reaching the toilet before the contents of my stomach spewed out.

Great. Just great.

After cleaning up, I tiptoed through the hallway to the kitchen back entrance. My bare feet hit cold pavement and I winced. It didn't matter. Grandma would kill me, but I'd rather go home shoeless than face anyone inside the house.

I stumbled, my fuzzy head struggling to focus in the cool of the night air.

I concentrated on walking forward, shivering and wrapping my arms around myself. The pavement was a cold reminder of what a bad idea running away in my bare feet was. I had more than two miles to walk. In a T-shirt and jeans and no shoes.

Stupid. I didn't even have my cell. I'd left it in my backpack in Nathan's car. The lights from an oncoming car shone behind me. I hunched my shoulders, trying to be invisible and willing the driver not to notice me.

The headlights glowed bright. A surge of panic raced through me. The car slowed as it approached.

chapter five

The car pulled up beside me. I picked up my pace until I was on the verge of breaking into a run.

"Hey. Slow down. You're going to freeze to death," a voice yelled.

"Get lost," I snapped without looking up. Great. To top off my night, I'd be killed on the side of the road by a serial killer or something. I tried to remember if there'd been any reports of killers in the news.

"Hello? I'm trying to save you from freezing to death."

I recognized the voice.

"Jackson?" I stopped walking and peered into the driver's seat of the car. "What are you doing here?"

"I'm a regular knight," he said. "Come on, get in." He put the car in park.

I wrapped my arms around myself and shivered, but I didn't move.

Jackson stuck his head out the open window and peered at my feet. "You don't have shoes on. Come on. Get in the car."

"Congratulations," I told him. "You win the award as the most observant person on the planet."

My feet stayed firmly on the ground even though my mouth was flapping in the cold Washington wind. We hadn't had any snow in a while, and it was a pretty warm year, but the air was still cold.

He swore softly under his breath and then opened his car door, shot out to the road, and stood in front of me.

He put a hand gently on my back. "I'll take you home, okay?" He pushed, but I dug my toes into the cement, resisting him, and shook my head back and forth.

"You're not a very agreeable drunk," he said. "You're shoeless and freezing, so come on. Let's go." He guided me toward the passenger door. The warmth in the car tempted me. He opened the door for me and I scooted inside, wisely keeping my mouth shut, and stayed put.

He went around and slid inside the driver's door. When he got in, he pulled off his hoodie and handed it to me.

"Here," he said as he started the engine. "You look frozen."

I took the hoodie, hugging it close for warmth but not putting it on. It smelled clean. Not like Nathan and his cheap cologne. I hugged it tighter.

"I'm not drunk," I told Jackson and sneaked a look sideways at him. "Well, not anymore." My foggy brain felt sluggish but coherent.

He twirled his earring. "Your boyfriend is an idiot for letting you run around in the cold like this. And you must be drunk. I haven't heard you talk this much since I've known you."

I lowered my head, not bothering to inform him that Nathan was so not my boyfriend.

"You two have a fight?" he asked.

I shrugged, my teeth shivering from the cold. He reached down and blasted the heat, and I fought the urge to spill my guts. Babble to him about what I'd done. And why.

"How'd you find me?" I asked instead of answering.

Jackson shoulder-checked, but the road was empty, so he pulled the car out onto the road and drove on. "I saw you sneaking out the back door in your bare feet. And stumbling a little. So I followed you."

I leaned my head back and snuggled with his hoodie. I wanted to cry, but I knew that if I started, I wouldn't be able to stop. I pushed my teeth into my bottom lip and blinked quickly. "I didn't even know you were there," I mumbled.

"I just got off work and heard about the party so thought I'd pop by before I went home." He pointed to the floor in front of me.

I looked down. My black-and-white-checked running shoes were tucked at the back of the floor mat.

"How'd you know they were mine?"

"Lacey saw me searching the shoes and told me the sneakers were yours. I'm not Sherlock."

"Thanks," I mumbled and slid on the shoes, grateful he'd at least spared me the wrath of my grandma for losing my "ridiculously priced running shoes."

"So. Where do you live?"

I gave him my address and sank back against the seat, wishing I could disappear inside it.

"You shouldn't drink so much," Jackson said.

"I don't." I hiccuped, and a semi-hysterical laugh slipped out. "Well, not usually." I chewed my bottom lip.

He made a sound in his throat like he was clearing it. After a minute he spoke. "You're a little young, aren't you? For a party like Marnie's?"

"I go there all the time. I have friends." I swallowed tears again. Some friends. "How did you even know about Marnie's? You're young too." Anger raised my voice an octave.

"Me?" He grinned. "I have ways of finding things out. Besides, I'm eighteen, almost nineteen. That's the legal drinking age in Canada."

"We're not in Canada." I glared at him. "Did you go to Marnie's to deal?" I sucked in my breath. *Way to play it cool, Jaz.* My inhibitions about speaking my mind had apparently vanished. Luckily, instead of pulling over and pushing me out the door, he laughed. The high-pitched sound hooted from his lungs like an off-key horn.

"Ouch," he said. "You heard about my illustrious past. Afraid it's true, though. I have a record and everything."

I frowned. Was it still true? Did he mean he *was* there to deal drugs? "Is Marnie your girlfriend or something?" My brain was putting words in my mouth. And spitting them out loud.

I shuddered at a flash of her bedroom. Her bed. I closed my eyes, hating myself, and projected my disgust at Jackson. "She's old. And she seems slutty. But I guess that appeals to a boy like you."

He grabbed at his heart. "Whoa. What's that supposed to mean? A boy like me?"

I stared out at the darkness in front of us. The liquor swirling through my blood made me an ass. Marnie had never done anything to me. Neither had he.

"Nothing," I said. "Sorry," I mumbled as an afterthought. He didn't deserve my anger. It wasn't him I was mad at.

He chuckled, though. "She's not my type."

Yeah. True enough. I'd seen his type at the coffee shop. Blond. Giggly.

"Anyhow," he said. "You should talk. Nathan's not your type."

"Nathan is not my boyfriend," I clarified and blushed, wondering if Jackson knew I'd been in a bedroom with Nathan. I turned my head away and made a face at my reflection in the window. I couldn't wait to get home to shower and scrape every smell and memory from my skin.

"That right?" Jackson asked.

His eyebrows shot up and I imagined his awful thoughts about me and wanted to cry with shame.

"Did something happen?" he asked, his voice low. He sounded dangerous. "I mean, did Nathan do something…Is that why you left without your shoes?"

I leaned my head against the seat. "No. It's not what you think."

I'd set myself up by drinking so much and letting Nathan kiss me. I'd led him on. Given him the wrong idea. I'd acted like an irresponsible idiot.

"You sure?"

Jackson sounded as if it actually mattered. I turned my head and fixed my gaze on the blackness outside the passenger window. "Why would you even care?"

I saw him glance at me in the reflection of my window and stared the other way, afraid he was making fun of me. "I thought we were kind of friends," he said. "Work buddies and all. Why wouldn't I care? You're sweet."

I thought about what I'd done with Nathan. "I am *not* sweet," I told him.

"Uh. A little prickly sometimes, but I sense marshmallow underneath," he said.

"I don't want to talk about this."

Jackson took me literally and stopped talking. We drove quietly for a while, and the stillness and dark soothed me. I almost felt like I was dreaming.

"Your grandma going to kill you?" Jackson finally asked.

"No. I mean, not since you saved my shoes and all. She doesn't wait up for me."

He nodded. "She's cool? About you going to parties?"

"Like I said, I don't usually drink, so she doesn't mind." I snorted softly. "I don't have a lot of friends at school, so she's happy I have a social life. She trusts me."

He stayed quiet.

"I know how hard it can be," he said, shattering the silence again. His voice was deep but almost gentle. "Growing up without your parents."

I rubbed my charm between my fingers and snuck a sideways glance at him. "What do you mean?"

"Just that I get it. I mean, I heard. That you never knew your dad."

I bristled at the mention of the Sperminator. "Really? You want to talk about him? He's not a dad. He's some stupid asshole who supplied sperm. How do you even know about 'my dad'?" Liquor brought words to the surface that I usually kept buried deep inside.

Another reason to never drink again. I clenched my teeth hard to keep my mouth shut.

"The same way you know things about me. My illustrious past. People talk. Anyhow, I understand more than you think. "

I sniffled. What did Jackson know about how it felt?

"I never knew my dad," he said softly. "But from what I heard, he was an asshole, so I'm okay with it, but still. It sucks. And you have the whole race thing to deal with too."

I held my breath, not quite believing he was going there. People never went there.

"Are there any other people in your life? Black people, I mean. Like grandparents or aunts or uncles or something?" Jackson asked.

My laugh was bitter. "That whole side of my family doesn't even acknowledge I exist so…um, no," I snapped.

He stayed quiet for a minute. "It's hard. Being the only one."

"There are other black people in town. That's how I got there, after all."

"I know that. I meant in the family. And you're the only biracial girl at Westwind. So you're kind of alone there too."

I snorted. "Thanks for noticing."

He glanced over and raised his eyebrows before looking back to the road. I lifted a finger to my mouth and started chewing on a hangnail.

"I notice things. I like to think I look a little deeper."

I glanced at his profile, envious of his thin nose. I'd always hated my wider nose, sure God gave it to me to remind me I was partially black. I tried to imagine his life for a moment, but I was too wrapped up in my own misery.

"I hate when people make snap judgments. Hate it."

Something inside me cracked a little. The darkness around us hugged me like a blanket, making me feel secure and more intimate with him.

"I don't give a crap who someone's parents are or what they do for a living," he added, and the blanket of darkness tugged at me.

"My life is a mess," I blurted out, surprising myself.

I looked over to see if he'd laugh or mock me. He just nodded.

"In high school, my mom was the blond princess, and my dad was the football star. A total cliché except that he was black. Back then it mattered even more than it does now. My mom, the rebel. Anyhow, they didn't go out for very long before she got pregnant. Grandpa told me my dad, I mean the Sperminator, didn't want her to have the baby. Me."

Grandpa had never sugarcoated his words. He was a strong believer in truth. He tried to make up for the fact that my father had never wanted me born by loving me more, but he'd always told me the truth about my birth.

"My father's family moved away before I was born. They didn't want to ruin the Sperminator's chance at playing college football. They never contacted me. They pretend I don't exist. I've never spoken with any of them."

Jackson nodded and glanced at me. I didn't see pity in his eyes before his gaze went back to the road. It was something else. And because he wasn't feeling sorry for me and because I was filled with liquor, I kept talking.

"My grandparents raised me. My mom lived with us too, but

we were more like sisters. Anyhow. We all did fine. I mean, my grandparents were great, but obviously they didn't know anything about being black. I looked the part but didn't have anyone to talk to about it. Well, until Simon came along."

"Simon?" Jackson asked.

I lowered my head, studying my shoes. "Simon has been my mom's boyfriend for about five years. He's black. We used to be kind of close."

"Used to be?"

I ripped off the skin from my hangnail with my teeth and it hurt, but in a different way than the pain inside me.

"It changed. My mom is pregnant, and Simon..." I thought about Lacey. An image of her kissing Simon flashed in my mind. Her arms wrapped around his. His mouth all over hers. I leaned my head back against the seat. "It's nothing." I closed my eyes tight to chase away the image. "We don't get along anymore."

"Did something happen? With you and Simon?"

"Oh, my God, no!" My eyes flew open, and I shivered.

"Sorry," he said softly. "You just looked really...freaked."

"It was nothing like that. Never mind. It was just...a stupid fight," I lied. "It doesn't matter." I turned my head and stared at the blackness outside. There were a few cars on the street, and the streetlights shone bright, but it seemed like most of the population of Tadita was home in bed.

"Okay." Jackson didn't sound convinced, but he reached for his radio dial and turned up the volume. "You're the boss," he said. "More rock. Less talk."

He flipped channels until a Neil Diamond song blasted over the speakers. "A classic." Jackson whistled along with the melody for a minute and then belted out the chorus, his voice surprisingly good. "Sweet Caroline," he sang.

"Dun dun dun." I couldn't resist adding that and then giggled.

Jackson glanced sideways. "You making fun of my voice?" he asked in mock anger.

"No." I signaled at the radio. "My grandpa loved this song. I mean, I love it too," I admitted.

"You know this is some hokey-ass music. But wait, didn't I hear you playing Neil Diamond when you were busking?"

"I wasn't busking." A smile curled my lip up.

Jackson made a sound that could have been a laugh. "That's what you claim." He turned the volume down so we could hear each other better. "I think you should seriously quit busking and join a band. Although finding a band that plays Neil Diamond may be tough." He smiled. "You take lessons?"

I glanced down at my lap. "No. My grandpa taught me. He died. My grandpa, I mean. He was the greatest guitar player I knew."

I looked up and Jackson nodded, his eyes still on the road. He pulled the car to a stop at a stop sign. "I think it's cool. That you carry your guitar around and jam when the mood strikes you. Like at school and at the park."

"Most people think it's weird. Think I'm weird."

"Yeah. Well, I'm not most people."

"Apparently not." I glanced at the four-way stop. There were no cars, but he didn't pull forward yet. "I can't believe you like Neil Diamond," I said.

"I can't believe *you* like him." He grinned. "Like I said, people really aren't always what they seem, right?"

True enough.

Jackson reached over and touched my hand for a second and then pulled back. "You know, I'm still pretty new around here. I mean, I don't have a lot of people to talk to. So, if you ever want to talk more, I'm game."

I laughed. "I don't normally talk very much."

"Maybe you just never had the right person to talk to."

A car honked behind us, and we both glanced back, surprised to see someone had pulled up behind us.

"Chill," Jackson said to the driver behind him as if he could hear. He looked at me and laughed. "What's with the face?"

"No face," I said. He was easy to talk to, but I'd also consumed more alcohol this one night than the rest of my life combined. "It's just that I haven't got a lot of friends. Especially male ones."

"No? Well, their loss. How about a rain check?" he pulled away from the stop sign. "You ever want to talk, there's no expiration date. Just let me know. Cool?"

Knowing I'd never take him up on it, I nodded. "Sure."

Jackson turned his car down my street then, and when I pointed to my house, he pulled in front. He shifted the car into park and idled.

I undid my seat belt and reached for the door. Before I opened it, I swallowed hard and let out a big breath. "Um. Thanks. For getting my shoes. And for the ride. You saved me in more ways than one." I handed his hoodie back to him.

"Take it," he told me. "It's cold outside."

"No. It's okay."

"I insist. And please keep being weird and playing Neil Diamond on your guitar."

He smiled, and I hugged the hoodie tight and then tugged on the door handle. "You know, you're not really the bad boy everyone says you are."

He laughed again, and it sounded like a horn. Weird, but somehow the geeky laugh made me like him a little more.

"Don't be so sure," he said. "But I'll take that as a compliment." He grinned.

I pulled his hoodie close to fight off the cold and inhaled the hoodie's smell. Boy smell. I liked it.

"You really did go to juvie for drug dealing?" I asked.

He lifted a shoulder. He didn't look proud or sorry. Accepting maybe. "Some rumors are true, I guess."

"I guess." I slammed the door behind me and wanted to climb back inside his car almost immediately. Mistakes seemed easier to forgive in there. I wondered if he was in danger of going back to juvie. I didn't want him to leave.

Instead of opening the car door to ask him or beg him to stop, I headed up the driveway. Back to real life.

Where mistakes mattered.

chapter six

Sitting up made my head feel like it might explode, so I rolled over and reached for the phone beside my bed. For the first time, I called in sick to work. At least it wasn't another lie. Inhaling coffee fumes all day would have made me throw up

I also couldn't risk Nathan showing up at Grinds and giving me knowing looks. I'd rather die alone in my room than face him. I rolled over on top of a lump and grabbed it, pulling it out from under the covers. Jackson's hoodie. Mortified at all the babbling I'd done with him, I nonetheless sniffed the hoodie, hugged it, and lay back down, falling back to sleep with my arms around it.

"Jasmine. You can't sleep all day. It's way past noon." Grandma poked her head in my room, but she didn't come inside. Her voice woke me from a sleepless dream. It could have been hours or minutes later.

"Flu," I croaked and made a pitiful face. I peeked at the clock beside my bed. It was almost two.

Grandma lifted her nose and sniffed the air. "Flu, my butt," she said in a most un-old-lady-like way. "Get up." She closed the door quietly behind her.

I groaned, not wanting to wake up and face myself and what I'd done the night before. I stared at the posters on my wall. Johnny Cash. Janis Joplin. Neil Diamond. They all stared down at me as if asking the same question.

What would Neil do?

Well, for sure he wouldn't have gotten into such a mess, making out with Nathan and needing to be rescued shoeless by Jackson.

I closed my eyes and tried thinking about the song lyrics I'd been working on for the past few days. Usually writing songs in my head soothed me, but my brain hurt too much to concentrate.

Outside my room I heard the landline ring, and a few minutes later the door opened.

"Your mom called," Grandma said, stepping through the doorway. "She told me she's been asking you out for dinner with Simon, and you keep making excuses." She crossed her arms, pulling her rose cardigan around her tiny body. "I told her you'd meet her and Simon tonight. You're meeting her at Pasta de Resistance at five." Grandma leaned against the door. "Get out of bed."

I lay back. "I don't want to go for dinner. I feel terrible." I lifted my arm and draped it across my eyes.

"Too bad." I didn't hear her budge from the doorway.

I moved my arm away to glare at her. "Fine. I'm getting up." My voice made me sound like an angry little kid, and I covered my face with my arm again.

Grandma clicked her tongue on the roof of her mouth. "Lacey also called. She's got your backpack. She wanted to make sure you made it home okay, which I assured her you did. Now get up and shower before I change my mind and ground you."

"Okay, okay. I'll go, I'll go." I sat up slowly, holding on to my head. I glanced at Grandma. "Headache," I said.

Usually she preferred old-fashioned cheek turning. She'd rather put on a pot of tea and talk about the weather than deal with stuff like this. Her lips disappeared into a straight line, but it had always been Grandpa's job to talk to me about serious stuff.

"You were drinking last night," she said. Great. Suddenly she wanted confrontation instead of tea. Perfect timing.

"Um." I looked her in the eye. "I only drank a little." The lie rolled off my tongue as if I'd been lying to her for years. I remembered being a kid and thinking she could read my mind. Except about the pool. She hadn't read my mind on that one. I'd been thankful for that.

She sighed. "You haven't forgotten the things you promised Grandpa, have you, Jasmine?"

I rubbed my eyes. I shook my head slowly so as not to hurt my brain. Grandpa wouldn't have let me get away with any of this. He would have been furious at me for taking advantage of the freedom they gave me and getting drunk.

"Jasmine." Grandma pressed her lips together again. "I'm not clueless about what goes on with kids your age, but I've always trusted you to make good decisions. Safe sex. That's why I let you stay out late. I don't want you sneaking around."

"Grandma!" I did not want to have *that* conversation. Especially after last night when I'd actually gotten close to a member of the opposite sex for the first time in my life.

"Well, how do you think you ended up being born?" she said in a crisp voice. "Osmosis?"

"I know, I know. Leave me alone, okay? I'm not having sex." Especially not with Nathan.

She didn't take her eyes off me. "Well, okay. But drinking will lead to bad decisions. You're only seventeen."

"Almost eighteen."

Grandma gave me a look, and I shut my mouth. "Lacey is old enough to drink, but you're not. You know I like her. But if you're going to get into trouble…"

Grandma let me hang with Lacey because it made both of us feel better that I had friends. Even if they were older.

"It wasn't Lacey's fault." I chewed the inside of my cheek. "I mean, she didn't make me drink." Not directly. I sat up and pulled my knees in close, trying to make myself smaller.

"You have a mind of your own. I'm aware of that, but I worry about you. It's my job. Now up. Shower. Out of bed. It's not okay to hang around in bed all day." She paused. "Drinking makes people do stupid things."

"Like getting pregnant?" I asked.

Grandma crossed her arms and pressed her lips tighter.

"Well, if Mom hadn't gotten pregnant, I wouldn't even be here for you to worry about."

Grandma stepped closer. "That's not what I mean. We were blessed with you." She cleared her throat. "If something is bothering you, you can talk to me, you know. Like you did with Grandpa. It's not like you to drink. Is it?"

"No. Everything's fine." I stared past her shoulder at a poster. "It was stupid. I'm sorry. I won't get drunk again. I hated it. I feel terrible." I sighed. "I miss Grandpa."

"Me too." Grandma's cheeks reddened. Her tongue darted out to wet her lips. She needed to reapply her lipstick; she hated being without it. "Why don't you talk to Simon?"

"I don't want to talk to him."

Grandma's expression changed and she looked almost puzzled. "You're still angry with him? You two have such a bond. I've loved that."

"You mean because we're black?" I snapped.

"Well, no." Grandma hesitated and sat on the edge of my bed. "You're not just black. You're white too, right?" She reached out and stroked my arm.

"No, Grandma. You're white." I hugged my knees tighter. "I've never really been considered white by anyone except you and Grandpa."

"That's not true." Grandma clucked her tongue like a rooster on speed.

"It is. I mean, let's face it. Tadita is a pretty conservative town. Black people stick together, and white people stick together. I feel like the monkey in the middle sometimes." I rested my head on top of my knees and struggled against the feelings whirling inside me. I'd never told her or Grandpa about the day at the pool. I never would.

"You and Grandpa always said I needed to accept myself for who I am. But I never knew parts of myself. I still don't."

She reached for my knee and held on.

"You didn't teach me about being black. You didn't even know how to do my hair," I said. "I looked like Mickey Mouse for the first seven years of my life."

Grandma started to laugh, and I couldn't help it, I joined her. I'd had the worst rat's nest as a kid. She'd tugged at it and messed around with it and usually put it in pigtails. Two round clumps of coarse hair that sprouted from the sides of my head.

Then she'd tried cutting it really short, Afro style, and I cried about it so much she let me grow it out. Finally she'd started sending me to the black hairstylist in town.

I did my own hair now. I was pretty good at it too. A skill I'd been forced to acquire. Spiral curls were easier with good hair products like the Mixed Chicks gel I bought on eBay.

"Oh, God, your hair," she said, giggling, and then she sobered up.

"I'm sorry." She sighed heavily and took her hand from my knee and patted her gray hair. "I didn't know what to tell you. I just wanted you to be proud of who *you* are."

She tugged on her ear. "Does it matter, Jasmine?" she finally asked. "What other people see? You're half white too."

"It matters," I told her. How could it not? "And my father's family, they never even acknowledged me. Not even when I was a little baby."

"I know. And I'm sorry. But it's their loss, you know. We always wanted you to believe that. They missed out. Oh, did they miss out." Grandma sighed. "You are the most beautiful child. Inside and out."

I stared at my bed. "That's easy for you to say."

She had no idea what it was like not to know where she belonged. No matter how white or how black I was, it seemed like neither was enough.

"I know. I know it is." She stroked my arm. "Don't think I never saw the way some people looked at us when you were growing up. Some of them still do. I know that." She pressed her lips together. "It still makes me angry. Sometimes I wanted to slap people for their ignorance."

I couldn't help grinning at that image. My do-good, volunteer-addicted grandmother slapping people around for looking at me funny.

"I'm sorry, honey. I didn't know what to do. I never knew how to help with the black part. I left it up to your grandpa, and I don't suppose he did much either. I wish we'd done more. That's why when Simon showed up and stuck around..." her voice trailed off.

I bit my lip, not wanting to think about Simon. "Remember when you gave me that black doll when I was a kid? That Cabbage Patchy thing."

She groaned. "You hated it. You threw her in the garbage and pretended it was an accident."

I bit my lip. "It was different from the other dolls girls were playing with."

"So were you, I guess. Different." She patted me as if I were a little dog or cat. "Maybe we should have moved to a place where there are more kids like you. More mixed couples with kids."

I held my breath, overwhelmed. She'd never said anything like that to me before. Never.

"Well, Grandpa loved Tadita." Washington was in Grandpa's blood, he'd said. Especially the wide-open spaces right outside our town. We spent a lot of time hiking the mountains, and even now when I needed to put my life in perspective, a trip to the mountains with a pair of hiking boots did wonders. I should have hiked instead of going to Marnie's stupid party.

"Grandpa knew as much as I did about being black or African American or whatever the polite term is these days. I don't know why I thought he'd be any better at explaining than me."

I smirked. "Well, he made sure I had a great background in blues history. And he got me lots of CDs. Even though he ended up teaching me rock and roll." I glanced over at my guitar leaning against the wall and the posters of white rock-and-roll stars on my walls. Something else I loved that set me apart from the few black kids I knew in Tadita.

Grandma reached up to cover her smile. The skin on her hand was thin and spotted. "He tried. We both tried." She lowered her hand, her smile gone. "But really, what did we know about anything?"

"Grandpa was my dad," I said. "In the ways that mattered."

"I know, sweetie." She sighed. "Is that what's causing problems with you and Simon? That he's sticking around for the baby? And the man that fathered you didn't?"

My nostalgic feelings vanished. My headache returned full force. "That has nothing to do with it, Grandma. Trust me."

She took a deep breath and blew it out. It disappeared like a note fading out.

"Try reaching out to Simon. He's a good man. He's good with

you." She stood. "And don't you dare go out and get drunk again. There'd better not be a next time. Not until you're thirty."

She shook a finger at me. "Now. You go have a shower and clean yourself off, and then go and meet your mom for dinner."

• • •

Pasta de Resistance buzzed with life. The smell of Italian food and spices mingled with the noise, making my head ring and my stomach queasy. Usually I loved the atmosphere, the loud music, and the clanking sounds of the restaurant, but tonight it was too much.

I stared across the red-checkered tablecloth at Mom's bloated stomach. It poked out of her loose maternity dress. I'd thought she'd pull off pregnant better. Her normally glowing skin was blotchy. She looked puffy and uncomfortable. Her disposition wasn't exactly radiant either.

Mom used the back of her hand to wipe sweat off her brow and then glanced at her watch for about the hundredth time. "I can't believe Simon. He's always late. I told him 6:30, and it's quarter to seven already." She glanced around as if she was about to cry.

Her moods were getting darker as her stomach got bigger. She didn't usually complain about Simon.

I picked up a glass of water and took a sip. "He's not that late," I said and put my glass down.

Secretly I wished he'd leave us waiting all night long. I envisioned him disappearing into thin air, like one of those men who go out one night to buy a pack of cigarettes and never return. Too bad Simon didn't smoke.

"What would you do if Simon didn't want the baby?" I asked.

"What?" her eyes flashed. "What are you talking about? Did he say something to you?"

A waiter walked by carrying a huge tray of drinks, and my stomach rolled in protest.

"Of course not. I haven't talked to him about it. No, I just meant, you know, what if you ended up bringing up this baby by yourself?"

"This isn't the same. Your father wanted nothing to do with you." The wrinkles in her forehead deepened. No Botox with a baby on the way.

I leaned farther back in my chair, putting more distance between us. I changed my mind, wishing Simon would appear. And soon.

"Sorry. I didn't mean it like that. I just meant that Michael didn't want a baby. We were so young. It had nothing to do with you."

"Uh. It had everything to do with me." I picked up my water glass, sucked up a couple of ice cubes, and crunched them, chewing rudely. How could she think it had nothing to do with me?

"Michael was the same age as you are now, for God's sake. He had plans. College. Football. We weren't even serious. I was the one who chose to have you. I knew I was on my own." She glanced around the restaurant. "And Grandma and Grandpa wanted to keep you so badly too. They told me they would raise you. They did so much better than I could have. But this is different. I'm older now. Simon wants our baby. He'll be there for this baby." She leaned back in her chair with her hands folded protectively over her stomach.

"Unlike my 'father.'" I had an urge to put my head down on the table and close my eyes. I tried not to think about him much. Daddy. Now I'd thought about him twice in one day.

"It's complicated," Mom said.

"Not really."

"He did set you up a trust fund. I didn't ask him to do that. He did it on his own. He gave you a secure future."

Yeah, a few years after he married his college sweetheart, the Sperminator must have gotten a dose of the guilts or something. He'd dumped money in an account for me, the one and only time he'd ever acknowledged his part in my existence. All he'd asked for in a letter written to my mom was that I not contact him. Isn't that what they called hush money?

"So I should be grateful? He paid me off so he doesn't ever have to advertise his half-white daughter. Or the blond he knocked up. Mighty big of him, I'd say."

I'd googled him last year in a moment of weakness. He was some sort of business guru now. Used his football scholarship well, apparently, after he'd blown out his knee his final year. He owned property all over the place. The black woman he'd married, his college sweetheart, ran her own real-estate business. They'd had two little girls. A picture of the couple appeared on the home page of his website. Tall, dark, and beautiful. Happy and perfect. Smiling. His profile said they met at college. She'd been in the same year as him and had majored in business. They'd graduated together. Married and had babies right on schedule.

I wondered if she even knew I existed, his half-mocha daughter. I wondered if his kids knew they had a half sister. Half blood. Half sister. Half white. I wondered if they'd care someday.

Mom sighed, and the waiter hovered closer to our table, not even trying to pretend he wasn't eavesdropping. She flicked her hand in the air, waving him away, and he slowly moved along. She clenched her jaws, her resolve hardening like an old man's arteries.

"I can't change what happened or who your father is. I thought we'd dealt with it."

I snorted. "You thought we'd dealt with it? I'm the one with the father who bought me off with a deposit in a bank account. You had the best father in the world, and you didn't even tell him. Grandpa Joe would have done anything for you. He did do anything. He became a father to your own child."

"Hey, ladies, sorry I'm late."

It figured Simon would pick that moment to swoop up to the table. He looked back and forth at us, his big charming smile fading a little. "Did I miss something?"

"A condom?" I said.

His lips turned down. His eyes had bags under them. Maybe I wasn't the only one at the table suffering from a hangover.

"If I didn't know better, I'd think you actually didn't like me anymore, Jaz." He smiled, but it wasn't sincere. "But you're a teenager, so I'll pretend you do. You look nice. Cute dress. I like that color on you."

His condescending smile made me sick. I'd only worn the dress to try to please Grandma. I hated it. More now. Simon looked hipper than me in his T-shirt and jeans. A couple of teenage girls at the table next to us actually ogled him.

Simon completely ignored the obvious tension at our table. He joked and touched Mom a few times as he babbled. I stared through him, hating his handsome face, hating his gift of gab. Hating the way he played her. I knew that he'd already done something to hurt her. With Lacey. I just didn't know how far they'd gone.

"God. I wish I could have a drink," Mom said when he finally paused for a breath.

"Go ahead," I snapped. "It's not like you're getting nominated for a Mother of the Year award."

In the background people talked and cutlery clinked. The silence at our table was louder.

"Hey," Simon said. "Your mom wouldn't drink in her condition. She's going to be a great mom. She already is." He reached out and stroked her hand.

I wanted to barf.

"How do you know?" Mom asked and pulled away. "I didn't even raise her." She pointed at me. "She doesn't even like me."

I stared down at the table and forced myself not to apologize or reassure her. I loved her, but right then I didn't care. Why should I be the only one who hurt?

"That was different," Simon said. "You were very young. And you've always been there for Jaz. You have a great relationship." I glanced up. He shot a look at me that made my insides wince, but I didn't flinch.

"Appreciate that you still have your mom around to talk to, Jaz. I miss my mom every single day."

Mom sniffled. Simon opened his eyes wider, trying to send me a message, but I ignored him. I was sorry his mom had died, but that had nothing to do with my situation.

The waiter stepped into our space. Must be a slow night because he seemed to be enjoying the show. Simon ordered a beer, and the waiter went to get it.

"Hair of the dog?" I asked politely.

"What? The beer? Nah. I'm too old to get drunk anymore." He sheepishly glanced at Mom. "Well, maybe once in a while, like the night I found out I was becoming a dad."

Yeah. I'd seen him drunk, his lips all over my best friend.

"Anyways. I heard you were the one having a good time last night." He wiggled his eyebrows. "Nathan your new boyfriend?"

"No. He is not." I willed him to shut his mouth.

He grinned. "Damien said Nathan had his arm around you at a party, that's all." He winked. "Oh, and there might have been some kissing."

I almost passed out with embarrassment.

"Really?" Mom asked, finally looking interested in something other than her own misery. "Is that true?" She sat up and her grumpy expression softened.

I narrowed my eyes. The last thing I wanted to talk about was Nathan. "Tell Damien to mind his own business. Just because he's your brother doesn't mean he gets to spy on me."

Simon held up his hands. "Hey. Sorry, kid. I was just having some fun with you."

"Nathan's that skinny kid who lives with Lacey? Isn't he a little old for you? He doesn't seem like your type."

I scrunched my nose. "I don't have a type. Unlike you, I'm not addicted to a color." I reached for my water and took a sip. I did not want to be having this conversation.

"Hey, your mother's taste in men is awesome." Simon grinned. "Once you go black, you never go back."

"Gross."

"Jaz." Mom sounded amused. "It's okay to have fun at your age. Boyfriends are normal. Just be careful."

I squeezed my eyes closed and covered my ears. "Shut up!"

"Hey." Mom threw her napkin at my head.

I fumed.

"We're only teasing." Her brows furrowed.

"You've been mad at me since you found out your mom and me are having a baby." Simon reached over and folded a hand over Mom's. She didn't pull away.

"You're an important part of the baby's life, Jaz. A big sister. I'm not going to come between you and your mom." He spoke in a soothing tone, as if I were a child.

I snorted. He already had. I pushed back on the chair and stood. I turned to my mom. "I could not care less about you or your stupid baby. I feel sorry for it. You're the worst mother in the world. And, Simon, bite me."

I rushed from the table. My best high heels flapped on my feet as I scooted past people eating dinner and looking up at me surprised. I fled the restaurant, afraid that if I turned back and saw my mom's expression, I'd run back to say I was sorry, that I didn't mean it. But if I turned back, I might blurt out what I'd seen. Instead, I ran. Again.

chapter seven

Ashley shifted the stick shift on her car and glanced at me. A truck sped past us in the other lane, bright lights momentarily blinding me. The flash of the headlights lit up the purple tips of her hair.

"Thanks for picking me up," I said.

Thank God, she'd been home. I'd been nervous calling her since, until now, we hadn't had the "I'm stranded. Can you pick me up on the side of the road?" kind of friendship. But she was the only person I could think of, and I'd been close to her neighborhood. She'd said she'd come without even hesitating.

"No big deal. Not like I was all booked up on a Sunday night. Homework can wait, and you sounded kind of desperate. What's up?"

I leaned my head against the window of her car. "God. My freakin' life is a mess."

"Welcome to the club," she said, but she grinned. "You want to talk about it?"

I sighed, not unaware that this was my second deep conversation inside a car in as many days. I wanted to talk about it. But I couldn't.

"Not really."

She nodded and didn't pry. Ashley was good that way. She didn't try to force things out of me if I didn't want to share.

"So. Where to?" she asked.

I shook my head, unable to decide. I didn't want to go home yet. Grandma would have too many questions.

"I had a fight with my mom and Simon," I said instead of coming up with a destination. I watched out the window as we passed by the other high school, the one with the state champion football team. The school Ashley used to go to until they managed to chase her out. The pool she swam at stood beside it. The same pool from fourth grade. I looked away.

When I didn't say more, Ashley spoke. "I hate fighting with my dad. But it happens all the time."

I knew Ashley's mom had died of breast cancer seven or so years back, but she didn't like to talk about her mom any more than I liked to talk about my dad.

"Yeah? How come?" I asked.

"He has a hard time. You know. With me being gay. He struggles with it. I used to be his little princess. That's what he thought anyway. He didn't know his princess was hoping that the frog she was kissing would turn out to be a beautiful princess instead of a prince."

I laughed and Ashley did too. But then she fell silent as we pulled up to a red light. "I can't bring home my girlfriend. He won't deal with it."

"You have a girlfriend?"

The light changed, and she glanced at me again before her eyes went to the road and she put her foot on the gas. "Marnie O'Reilly."

I gasped out loud. "Marnie is *gay?*" I shouted.

Ashley laughed. "Apparently."

"Holy cow, I had no idea," I sputtered stupidly.

Luckily Ashley wasn't offended. "Marnie is pretty private. We don't advertise."

I nodded, still blown away. Thinking about it, I'd never seen Marnie with a guy. Another person I thought I'd known but didn't know at all. "So why weren't you at her party last night?"

"After swim practice I had to go to a dinner thing with my dad and his girlfriend. Keep up appearances, you know. He likes to pretend we're fine."

I nodded. I didn't want to tell her about my night at Marnie's. Or about Nathan.

"What about you?" she said as if she'd read my mind. "You seeing anyone?"

I snorted but an image of Jackson's face appeared in my head. "As if," I said.

"As if what?" she asked.

"Who'd want to go out with me?"

"You're kidding, right?" she asked.

I didn't say anything. We pulled up to another set of lights, and Ashley stopped but then flipped on her blinker and turned right. I had no idea where we were going.

"With that gorgeous hair, that face, and those eyes?"

"You have no idea how much each of those qualities has

tormented me since birth." My eyes were a funny color. Not dark brown or even green. Rusty. Like a rotting old car.

"You want to go for coffee somewhere?" I asked to change the topic. I looked out on the streets. We were in a residential area but getting closer to farmland.

"Nah. I like to drive around when I'm in think mode. You mind?"

I shook my head. It was kind of nice, driving in the dark with nowhere to go or be.

"You realize you have some serious self-esteem issues," Ashley said.

I laughed, but I wiggled in my seat, uncomfortable. "Yeah. Well, you try being biracial in this town. No one wants anything to do with me." I tried to keep my voice light, as if it didn't matter. She turned down another street, and a group of young boys were playing hockey on the street. They pulled the net away from the middle of the road so we could pass.

Ashley made a noise in her throat. "That's not true. You keep people at a distance. You don't let anyone in. I mean, even me, and we're friends."

My blood boiled just a bit. "You don't have any idea," I told her. I glanced over my shoulder. The hockey game had resumed.

"So tell me," she said.

I bit my lip, wishing life was that simple still, and swiveled back around.

"You can talk to me. We're friends."

I smiled at that. I wanted to tell her, I did. My sanity was pretty much hanging by my chewed-up nails. I closed my eyes, struggling with the memories that wanted to stay buried.

"It's okay, Jaz."

My stomach fluttered and I took a deep breath, not sure if it was fear or excitement making me feel nauseous. I wanted to tell someone. Share my shame.

"Everyone stopped paying attention to me a long time ago." I closed my eyes, hearing the taunting voices from my past.

"What happened?" Ashley said softly.

I opened my eyes and looked at Ashley's profile. Her hazel eyes sparkled with compassion.

I wanted to trust her. Let her in. Tell someone what had happened. We drove to the end of the street and turned onto an unpaved road. Without streetlights it was spooky and darker.

"When I was in fourth grade, I almost drowned at the pool because of the efforts of the entire fourth grade. They wouldn't let me get to the side. And after that, they started ignoring me. I don't keep people at a distance. They stay there on their own."

"Your fourth-grade class almost drowned you?" Loose rocks sprayed the back bumper of Ashley's car, and she swore. "Stupid unpaved road."

She did a sudden U-turn, and we started back to the residential area. I stared out the window. "We were taking swimming lessons. The whole fourth grade. It was the last day. Free time. They started taunting me. It started out with a couple of kids, and then more came. A crowd mentality took over or something. Bullying at its finest, I guess. They trapped me in the middle and wouldn't let me get to the side while they chanted that my skin was dirtying up the pool. I slipped under and stopped breathing. The lifeguard had to resuscitate me."

We rolled over a bump and back onto the paved road.

"No wonder you're afraid of the water," Ashley said.

"You think?" I blinked away tears.

"That's horrible, Jaz."

"I've never told anyone before."

"You haven't? You never told your mom? Or your grandma?"

I shook my head. "It was hardest not to tell my grandpa. But it would have killed him. I was so ashamed. I felt like it was my fault."

"Well, what about later on? You never talked to a friend?" She didn't mention Lacey by name, but I knew who she meant.

"Lacey and I don't talk about stuff like that. I mean, we didn't. We're not really friends anymore."

"Yeah. I noticed that. What happened with you two?"

I lifted my thumb to my mouth and gnawed the calloused pad. "That I don't want to talk about."

Ashley didn't say anything. "I'm sorry about what happened to you. With those kids." She took her attention off the road for a second and glanced at me. "But do you want an honest observation?"

I shrugged. Ashley was all about telling the truth. Understandable after hiding it for so long, I guess.

"What they did was awful. But it was five or six years ago, right? Not that time makes it okay. But it seems to me that you play your part at keeping people away. I don't want to be a jerk, but not everyone at Westwind could have been a part of what happened, right? But you don't let anyone get close to you. Not even me. Not really. It's like you've built a wall around yourself. You're beautiful and smart and talented with your guitar and singing, but I think you use it to intimidate people. They think you're looking down your nose at them."

Her words stung, and I jumped in to defend myself. "You don't know what it's like. I'd always felt a little different, but I'd managed to fit in and have a few kids to play with. Until that day at the pool. They turned on me. Maybe they'd sensed my self-consciousness. My dark skin might have been more noticeable. Maybe they saw for the first time how different my hair was when it was wet. Maybe picking on me made them feel better about themselves. Whatever it was, it was awful."

"Um. I had to switch schools when I came out, remember?" she said. "Try being a lesbian with a high-pitched voice," she said and slowed down the car, flicked on her turn signal, and turned right onto a street with a kids' park on the corner. My face warmed. "Sorry." I sighed. "Pity party for one." I stared out the window as we drove past a row of brown and gray houses. They all looked the same. If I were a house on the street, I'd be painted an ugly color and wouldn't fit in. Then again Ashley would be yellow or maybe orange. I turned to her. "I have no idea what it would be like to be a lesbian with a high-pitched voice."

"Yeah, well. That's okay. I have that one covered. But I don't have any idea what it would be like to be half black and half white in a town like Tadita."

"True," I said and then laughed. "But what the hell does being a lesbian have to do with your high-pitched voice?"

Her face lit up with a grin. "I don't know. I think people expect me to sound like a man. It freaks them out that I don't." Her grin faded. “But tell me what’s it like,” she said. “Being biracial and not knowing your dad.”

“My mom moved out after she graduated from college. I stayed with my grandparents. I had my grandpa though. He made me feel like I was his gift. He told me he and my grandma wanted another child, but couldn’t have one until they got me.” I smiled at the memory of Grandpa’s serious face as he’d try to give me enough love to fill me up. “He said my mom loved me so much she let him and Grandma raise me, and it was the best thing that ever happened to him.”

“He sounds awesome.”

“He was. He tried so hard to fill the shoes of the man who didn’t want anything to do with me.”

“Bizarre,” Ashley said. “Not the typical family, I guess.”

“I guess.” It’s all I knew.

“The weirdest thing is having a whole line of people I’m related to by blood, but I don’t even know them. The black side of me.”

“That sucks.” Ashley sneaked a side glance at me, and I saw pity in her expression.

“I spent a lot of time in therapy as a kid, talking about it.” I grinned, but I wasn’t kidding. “Grandpa insisted.”

Ashley nodded, but she reached over and squeezed my hand. I squeezed back, and then she took back her hand, shoulder-checked, and turned down a back alley.

“I spent time in therapy too. My dad thought they might be able to talk me out of being gay.” She laughed. “Actually we spent most of the time talking about him.”

I laughed.

"I had one person who got me," Ashley said. Her voice cracked, and her eyes filled with tears. "My uncle." She blew out a breath and blinked a few times. "Remember that watch I misplaced at Marnie's?"

I nodded. "Yeah."

"It was his. He gave it to me when I was thirteen." She kept one hand on the wheel and slowed down the car as she reached around to her back pocket and pulled the watch out, stroking the face of the watch with her thumb. "He was gay. I mean, he never came out and announced it to me, but he had a live-in boyfriend, and he didn't hide that or how much they loved each other. His name was Grady, Uncle Grady. He was my mom's brother."

She sniffed, tucked the watch back in her pocket, and tapped the wheel with her fingers. "Dad didn't care for him much, but I loved him. When Mom was alive, we'd visit him, and later we kept in touch online when he moved to California. He worked as an animator on some big movies."

Tap. Tap. Tap. Her fingers went up and down on the steering wheel, tapping to a beat in her head.

"He died a few years ago. AIDS. We never had the chance to talk about me being gay, but I think he always knew. He said I was his favorite niece. My mom had three other brothers, and they all had kids too." We came to the end of the alley, and she put on her signal and turned onto a street leading to the older part of town.

"You see them?" I asked. I tried to imagine what it would be like to have a big, extended family. Nine cousins. It sounded pretty awesome.

"No. None of them. They're very conservative. Dad doesn't have much in common with them either. Besides, they live in Georgia, and without Mom, well, we don't visit. Probably just as well, given my so-called lifestyle choice." She smiled, but bitterness turned down the corners of my mouth.

Worlds away. In miles and beliefs.

"I'm sorry," I said. "The kids at your other high school sucked too."

"Yeah. But my swim team is awesome. They don't give a crap. They like me 'cause I swim fast." She grinned. "And I have you."

I nodded. "Yeah, you have me." I stared out the window at the tall, thick trees lining the streets. They looked so bare. No leaves this time of year. "I wish I had something like swimming."

"Well, you have your music," Ashley said.

"Yeah. But that's pretty solitary."

"Maybe you should join a band."

"I'm more the solo type, and I don't want to make music a job. I do it because I love it. Anyhow, the music I like is not conducive to bands."

"You don't want to become a rich and famous rock star?"

"That's the last thing I want. I play for me. It's my escape. I'm not much into sharing it with people. Especially not for money."

"Not yet. That might change."

"I doubt it. I never want it to be something I have to do, you know?"

"Not really. I have to swim all the time to stay competitive. Sometimes I'd just like to sit on the couch and watch TV."

"You would not."

"Probably not. I do like me some physical punishment."

Ashley kept driving, and both of us took turns talking and then listening. I didn't bring up my fight with Simon or my mom again. I didn't mention what had happened with Nathan or my ride home with Jackson. There were still a lot of things I didn't want to talk about with Ashley. But we had crossed a line into a deeper friendship. And it warmed my heart. I loved the feeling of having someone on my side. Someone off center and on the outside. Like me.

"You need to come swimming with me," Ashley said when she finally dropped me off at home. "Show yourself that you can."

"I can't." I looked out the window at the front-porch light Grandma had left on for me. "I'm afraid."

"I know. But I'll help you. You need to do it. So you don't have to be afraid anymore."

I shook my head.

"Well, when you're ready, you know where I am."

chapter eight

My mind wandered, refusing to concentrate on the test lying on the desk in front of me. I flicked my pencil up and down and glanced up, catching Jackson watching me. He flashed a smile. I swallowed a desire to stick my tongue out at him and then flushed, realizing I also had an urge to stick my tongue right inside his mouth. To kiss him.

Oh. My. God. What was wrong with me? I ducked my head quickly. How could I be fantasizing about that with Jackson after what had happened with Nathan?

I tried to focus on the exam and not squirm with embarrassment every time I remembered something I'd said to Jackson in his car, but even as I finished the last essay question, I knew I wouldn't be proud when the grades came back. I should have cared more, but I didn't.

The bell rang, and as Mr. Dustan got up to collect the papers from our desks, I scrambled to grab my backpack from under my chair. Feet walked up next to mine. Bigger feet, wearing Converse shoes. Upside down, I stared at them.

"So. You survived?" Jackson's deep voice asked.

I swallowed and sat up. I nodded and stood, pretending to be a lot calmer than I felt.

"Did you have a bad hangover?" Jackson asked.

It took a lot of muscles to force out a fake smile. "It wasn't too bad." I wondered if heads could explode from embarrassment. I considered running out of the room screaming. That might be less humiliating.

"Good."

Go away, I thought in my head. Go. Away.

He stayed. "They say the best way to avoid a hangover is to stay drunk. But I wouldn't suggest it for a lightweight like you."

"Probably not the best idea." I was a little too freaked for a witty comeback.

"Probably not."

"So?" he said as if he expected me to say more.

My heart thumped in my chest. I read tiny white words on his black shirt. His tight black shirt. His chest was awesome. I squinted to read: "Sometimes when I'm alone I google myself." I smiled and tried to make myself say something. Nothing.

"You working tonight?" he asked.

"Um. Yeah."

He nodded but didn't bolt to escape my lame conversational skills, probably sticking because he felt sorry for my dorky ass. At least when I was drunk I hadn't been afraid to talk. I heard giggling behind us and turned my head.

"Oh. What's this? Have we got ourselves a little interracial love match?" said Tina Fawcett, a nasty girl with huge boobs and a tiny IQ.

In first grade I'd invited her over for a play date when she first moved down the street from me. She'd come, but when I went to her house, she told me her father didn't want her playing with "someone like me." I'd gone home in tears. That was the first time I'd ever heard Grandpa swear. He told me to stay away from Tina, and I took his advice.

I remembered her voice screaming at the pool though. She had been one of the first to start the taunts, but I was lucky that she'd chosen to ignore me all these years since.

"Screw off," Jackson told Tina nonchalantly without even looking at her.

Tina opened her eyes wide, glancing at her friends, and then she stared at Jackson as if offering him a challenge. Boys weren't supposed to talk back to her. Her boobs were supposed to prevent that.

Jackson smiled at me, ignoring her. "Tell me you're not a freak too."

"You didn't hear?" I fought to match his calm as I zipped up my backpack, ignoring the girls eyeballing us. I stepped away from my desk, and Jackson stepped aside to give me room. "Apparently my skin makes me *dirty*." My heart pumped with my audacity. But talking to Ashley about almost drowning had made the memory fresher, and I wasn't a scared eleven-year-old anymore.

Tina didn't even flinch. "Now here's a match made in crack heaven," she spit out. "The druggie and the not-quite-black girl."

My heart tripped over itself, but Jackson didn't even glance her way. He leaned down and whispered in my ear. "Remember what I said about gossip and judging?" He spoke so close that I felt moisture on my ear and smelled peppermint gum on his breath. Goose bumps covered my arms. "She's not worth getting into it with."

I forced myself to take another step to put space between Jackson and myself so he wouldn't see my reaction to him. He winked and turned for the door. "I'm going this way. You coming?" He gestured right with his thumb.

"Just a minute." I pretended to search for something in the front of my backpack. Being left alone with Tina and her friends was better than walking with Jackson. "Go ahead. I'm going the other way."

He ignored Tina and her friends as if they were insignificant dust particles. "Sure you're okay?"

"Fine."

"Okay. I'll see you at work tonight." He hesitated and then shrugged and walked out of the classroom.

"You gettin' it on with the bad boy?" Tina demanded as soon as he was gone.

I ignored her and watched him disappear into the hallway, sort of wishing I was, and then tried to rid my brain of those thoughts.

"Are you?" she asked.

I jutted out my jaw and glared at Tina's smirking face. Her eyes flickered with disappointment when I didn't show outward signs of being intimidated. Inside, my nerves were jittering like crazy, but Grandpa and experience taught me well over the years.

"Never let 'em see you sweat, Jazzie. Stand tall. Never let 'em know what you're thinking."

I kept my expression neutral, knowing Tina thrived on weakness. She'd ignored me for years, but I knew she marched around the school treating people like crap and drumming up hours of business for local therapists. The school psychologist should pay her a commission. And she had the nerve to call Jackson the bad boy. Worst thing he'd probably done to her was refuse to kiss her ass.

"Am I trespassing on your property?" I asked sweetly. In the back of my head an alarm silently rang. Who did I think I was, taking on Tina? "Or maybe he wasn't interested."

Nadine, her follower, made a tiny squealing sound. "Oh, my God, she can talk," she said and giggled.

Tina glared at me. "Gross. I'm sure I'd get an STD just kissing him. Guys like him have been around, you know." Tina snapped her gum and jutted her hip out.

Please, even I knew Tina had slept with half the football team.

"Well, I guess you have something in common," I politely told her.

"Oh, my God. I can't believe she said that," Nadine shrieked.

Truthfully, I couldn't believe it either.

"You're one to talk. Hanging out with that slut Lacey Stevens." Tina glared at me. "She'll screw anything that moves."

So much for flying under the radar. I blinked, surprised and slightly alarmed. How did she even know Lacey? They didn't exactly hang in the same crowds. Did she know about Simon? Had someone else seen them?

Tina crossed her arms across her overdeveloped chest and sneered at me. "What's the matter? Cat got your tongue?"

"Why do you care who my friends are?" I asked.

Snap. Snap. She clacked her jaw, chomping on her gum. "Oh, please. Friends? And as if anyone cares about you."

"You did say she was talented," a girl said. Carly. I remembered holding hands with her at recess in second grade. Before it became social suicide to touch me. Or talk to me.

Tina shot her a death glance. "I said I would never act like I was cool and superior, showing off my singing and guitar like a friggin' busker looking for spare quarters. That's hardly a compliment." She glared at me.

"I guess you have no choice but to hang out with white trash like Lacey. No one around here has wanted anything to do with you since you almost drowned yourself. Oh. Except that lesbian. And now the juvenile delinquent. You're probably desperate enough to do both of them to keep them around." The girls around her laughed, but they sounded nervous. "You sure do know how to pick 'em. I guess you don't have a lot of choice. Half-breed and all. "

The hair on my arms rose. I stood straighter. Every inch of my body went into flight mode, even though I had several inches on Tina in her heels versus my flat sneakers. I took a deep breath. I wouldn't run. "You know nothing about me."

Or my color, I silently added.

She grinned. There was no friendliness in the smirk. "My sister told me you were fooling around with some black guy. Trust me, there's not a lot I don't know about people at this school." She smirked again as my head felt close to exploding with anger. "Even you.

"I heard he's cute. For a black guy." Tina flashed an evil grin. "You know what they say about black guys. I may consider giving it a try. Wouldn't be hard to take a man from you."

The girls giggled, all except Carly. She stared at Tina, frowning.

"What?" Tina said to her. "You know what they say about black guys. I'm not prejudiced."

My heart pounded as the girls swarmed off in their group. I watched them strut away, unable to utter a word. They were pretty. A blond, a redhead, and a brunette. Carly looked back at me and kind of grimaced.

God. Would I have been forced to hang out with them and pretend to believe what Tina believed if I'd had a white father? That a group of guys were all the same because of their color? Would I be shallow and judgmental and part of a stupid school clique?

People pretended my color wasn't what made me different. It was me, they said. I shut people out. Even Grandma and Grandpa said my skin didn't define me; it didn't matter. But obviously, it did.

I slowly made my way to the hallway. Carly was standing outside the door, waiting for me. Alone.

"Tina asked Jackson out," she said in a quiet voice. "He turned her down." She hugged her textbooks to her chest. "He likes you, and she knows it. She'll try and take it out on you. I'd be careful. She can be really mean."

I didn't say anything.

She started walking away and then stopped and turned back. "I think it's cool that you play guitar and write your own music," she said. "I've heard you sing. You have a lot of talent. Tina hates it. She's jealous. She thinks she's a great singer, but she couldn't even get a part in the senior musical. You should have gone out for it."

"I'm not the school-play type," I told her.

She bent her head. "I know."

She turned then but didn't move. Slowly she circled back. Her cheeks were red, and she took a deep breath. "I'm sorry. I know no one ever talks about what we did. But I've never forgotten it. I don't think anyone has."

My body froze in place. I dropped my gaze to the ground, wishing she would go away. Stop talking.

"I wanted to tell someone what happened to you. Back in elementary school. For a long time. But I was too afraid. I saw the way you were shunned. I'm sorry I was such a chicken. I've never forgotten." She spun back around and hurried away.

I didn't know if her confession made me feel better or worse.

• • •

I walked into Grinds early for my shift, repositioning my guitar case on my shoulder. I'd popped home after school and picked it up and stopped at the park to play some songs. Cold as it was in the park, playing cleared my head. My brain was swirling with old emotions better buried or picked away on my guitar strings.

I almost didn't pick up the guitar, remembering what Tina said, that I was trying to look cool. But I wasn't doing it to impress Tina or anyone else. Music kept me sane. Maybe the fact that it bugged her should cheer me up a little.

"So," Lacey called out in a singsong voice from a table in the café. "What's up with you and Nathan?"

"Nothing," I snapped to cover my embarrassment. "Nothing is up with me and Nathan," I repeated for emphasis.

"Is that right?" a deep voice asked. "I definitely thought something was up."

Nathan was slouched over a chair behind Lacey's. She opened her eyes wider and lifted her hands in a defenseless pose. "He made me," she mouthed.

I didn't see any restraints on her.

Nathan glared at me. "Why'd you take off on me? You ignored my calls all weekend too."

My stomach turned. I fought an urge to rush away. I didn't want to deal with Nathan, but I also didn't want him thinking we had something going on.

"My cell was out of juice. You didn't call my house," I stammered.

"Like I'd call your house. Your grandma would freak if she knew we were hooking up."

"We're not hooking up." My insides recoiled as if he'd asked me to perform live with him at a rap concert.

"Why not? I thought we were cool," he said as if we'd been more than drinks and hormones.

Was he serious? He thought we were an item? I sighed and plunked down in the seat beside Lacey and slid my guitar under the table.

"Sorry, Nathan." I breathed deep and searched my brain for words. "I drank too much. It was stupid. We're friends. Let's not get weird, okay? Can't we pretend it never happened?" I flashed a feeble smile and glimpsed at Lacey for help.

"Pretend it never happened?" Nathan pounded the table with his fist. "You weren't acting like a friend."

I shrunk down farther in my seat.

"Nathan. Chill," Lacey barked. "Leave her alone. She's a kid. She doesn't usually drink, and she's not experienced."

"She's experienced now." Nathan's voice sounded ugly.

I glared at him, the echo of my heart thumping loudly in my ears. I opened my mouth to defend myself when Jackson walked up to the table.

"Hey. How's it going?" He touched my arm, and something about it felt protective.

My skin tingled and my face burned.

"Hey," Jackson said to Lacey. He didn't greet Nathan.

"What do you want?" Nathan snarled.

"Relax, my friend." Jackson sat in the chair to my left. He raised his hand. "I come in peace."

Nathan slammed his fist down on the table again, so hard this time that it shook. "Screw you," he said to Jackson. "And screw you," he spit at Lacey. "And screw you too," he said to me. "Or maybe I already did?"

"You did not!" I yelped.

"Grow up." Lacey pointed to the exit of the coffee shop. "Get out of here until you cool off."

I glanced around the café. All eyes were on us. I wanted to crawl under the table.

"Amber'll ban you if you keep this up," Lacey told him.

Nathan leaped to his feet and gave her the finger. He glared down at me and stormed out of the café.

"Hmmm. I guess you're not on his Christmas list," Jackson said.

A loud laugh escaped my throat, like an unexpected hiccup.

Lacey crossed her arms over her chest. "Nathan's being an asshole because he feels rejected."

"Well, he must act like an asshole a lot then," Jackson quipped.

I giggled again but covered my mouth when Lacey scowled. I couldn't help it. My nerves, plus relief that he'd left, made me giddy.

"You know how he feels about you, Jaz. You shouldn't laugh at him," she said.

"How he feels?" I turned my nose up.

"He has a thing for Jaz," Lacey said to Jackson but her eyes stayed on me.

"He has a thing for every girl who breathes."

Jackson leaned across the table. "Hold your breath around him in the future," he whispered.

I ducked my head, but it was too late to hide my smile.

Lacey cleared her throat and tossed her hair over her shoulder. "I've gotta go get washed up before my shift." She stood. "Don't forget who your real friends are." She ignored Jackson and spun on her heels and walked away.

Jackson watched her go. "I guess that doesn't include me."

"She should talk." I chewed my lip, the light mood gone for good.

"I thought she was your BFF." Jackson made quote marks in the air.

"So did I. I was wrong."

He brushed his bangs out of his eyes. "So, how come you hang out with those two anyway?"

"Lacey is my best friend. Was my best friend," I corrected myself. "Nathan and her go way back. They're roommates."

"They're a lot older than you." He twirled his hoop earring as he studied me. "You really shouldn't mess around with him."

I ducked my head and kept my eyes on the table. "I'm not.

Anyhow, Lacey has been my friend since I was fourteen." I had an urge to cry. Because she wasn't my friend now. Not anymore. And Nathan wasn't my friend either. I wouldn't miss him though. He never really had been.

Jackson held out his hand. "All I'm saying is maybe you need some friends on the same page."

"I have Ashley."

He shrugged.

"She goes to our school. The swimmer. She hangs out at Marnie's too."

He nodded. "I've seen her around. I don't know her. "

I didn't want to explain further, so I pretended to study my nails. Easy for him to talk about making friends. He'd barely lived in Tadita six months and already got invited to parties. He probably made friends by dealing. It explained the calls on his cell.

"Nathan's not your type, and I don't mean because he's black."

I glared at him. "Nathan is not my boyfriend. And that has nothing to do with it."

"Good. He's too old for you."

He stared at me until I blushed and looked away.

"So who are you interested in then? Maybe you need a real boyfriend."

My stomach flipped, and my cheeks warmed. I prayed he couldn't tell my mind had conjured up a picture of him. Him as my boyfriend.

The trouble was that his voice sounded casual, almost brotherly, as if he was about to suggest setting me up on a blind date. Just what I needed. Love help from the juvenile delinquent I secretly crushed on. Man. I was seriously messed up.

Jackson pointed to my guitar. "How about someone who digs Neil Diamond?" He smiled and my heart actually hurt.

I leaped up, unable to sit still and listen to him trying to set me up. "We should get ready for work." I picked up my guitar case and slung it over my shoulder.

Jackson glanced at the clock on the wall. "Yup. I guess we should."

"It's not really your business, you know. Who my friends are."

He lifted his shoulder. "Fair enough. Just that I thought I was one, you know? Seems to me you're a girl who could use some laughs." He got to his feet and held out his hand. "After you."

I scooted past him a little too closely, and his hand brushed against the exposed part of my skin. A shiver tingled up and down my back, but thankfully he didn't seem to notice my reaction.

"Maybe you could play your guitar just for me someday," he said.

"Maybe you could hand over your next paycheck."

He laughed, but his cell rang, and he turned his back to me and answered it.

"Yeah. I got your stuff," I heard him say into the phone.

Great. Friends with a drug dealer. Grandpa had to be rolling in his grave. Again.

• • •

Over the next few weeks, Jackson and I worked a lot of the same shifts at Grinds. I wondered if it had anything to do with Amber's scheduling. She liked to nag me about needing more friends my own age and was probably stepping in. I liked talking to Jackson, but we had an unspoken agreement. Some things we didn't discuss. Lacey. Nathan. His phone calls that I suspected had to do with drugs. I ignored them because his offer of friendship had become a pseudo-reality. My first friendship with a boy.

I kept forgetting to bring his hoodie to work, and he eventually told me not to worry about it, and I kind of claimed it as my own. I didn't wear it, but I wrapped it on my shoulders to keep warm when playing guitar in my room.

I thought about inviting Ashley to hang at the coffee shop to show people I wasn't as bad off as everyone thought, but she had swim practices after school. Besides, I didn't want to subject her to Lacey's wrath.

Ashley invited me to swim with her, but that wasn't going to happen. She also asked me to hang with her and Marnie, but I didn't want to be a third wheel and said no.

Lacey's calls and pleas for forgiveness eventually tapered off. I never stayed for coffee with her or Nathan after work, and I didn't go to parties or hang at their house anymore. The time I used to spend with Lacey I spent alone playing the guitar. I wrote some new songs, driven by feelings I couldn't express any other way.

I kept my distance from my expanding Mom too, because when I saw her stomach, all I could think about was Simon. The secret ate away at me, but I couldn't do anything except keep it inside and hope that was the right thing to do. Sometimes I wished I'd never been at that party, that I'd never seen Simon and Lacey.

I wondered what was worse, knowing or not knowing?

chapter nine

My fingers strummed the strings of my guitar. I closed my eyes and bobbed my head, feeling the sound more than hearing it. I hummed, rolling new words to the melody over in my mind. I tried different versions of the chorus, playing the same chords over and over. I'd been composing and rewriting for weeks.

Then, forgetting about chord progressions or melody, I improvised a new sentence to see if I could open my mind and get it right. I didn't have it yet, but I trusted my process. It would come.

I strummed, searching the music and letting sound wash over me.

"I saw you there, exposing your lies."

The phone rang and I snarled at it, but Grandma had told me she was expecting a call, so I put down my guitar and leaned across my bed to pick it up.

"Jaz?"

"Hey, Mom." Damn. I'd been too out of it to check the call display.

"Hi, honey. I'm so glad I finally caught you. I haven't seen you in ages. You should see me. I'm huge. Bloated. I look like someone injected my entire body with helium. I think the baby dropped though…"

She went on and on about week thirty-four of her pregnancy,

describing new symptoms and ailments. In vivid detail. After she mentioned hemorrhoids, I tuned out until she said, "Will you go shopping with me? Take my mind off it?"

"Uh..." I tried to think of an excuse, but my mind was still too slow.

"Please," she begged until I agreed to meet her at the mall after work.

When I hung up, I picked my guitar back up but instead of my own song, I played Grandpa's favorite Neil Diamond song. The same song Jackson had sung the night he drove me home.

"Sweet Caroline," I sang and closed my eyes. The hole Grandpa had left throbbed in my heart, and I couldn't breathe properly for a second.

"Jasmine?"

I jumped at the sound of Grandma's voice and pulled my fingers off the strings almost guiltily.

"I didn't hear you come home." I put my guitar down on the bed.

"I just came from the church. I could really use your help."

"What's up?"

"There's an open volunteer spot," she said.

I waited. I'd heard a million variations over the years since Grandma retired from nursing. For as long as I could remember, I helped serve Thanksgiving dinners to the needy at the local church. At Christmas I helped put together food hampers. Then there were Grandpa Joe's impromptu concerts at the Senior Center and community fund-raisers Grandma volunteered us for.

"Our seniors group needs a volunteer on Wednesday nights.

Kind of a karaoke thing. They need someone to play guitar. The man who was supposed to handle it had a heart attack."

I wrinkled my nose, thinking how much I didn't want to play guitar for a bunch of off-key old people. "There's no one else?"

Grandma shook her head and pressed her lips tight, and I knew she wanted me.

I sighed. "All right. I'll talk to Amber about not scheduling me Wednesday nights."

"Thank you, sweetie." Grandma sat on my bed, her slight frame barely indenting the comforter beside me. "Are you working tonight?"

I nodded.

"Good. You can talk to her tonight." She smiled. "You could use some nights out. Other than work, I mean."

Things were pretty bad if Grandma thought a night out with senior citizens would do me good.

"I go out. I hang out with Ashley at school and I work."

"Hmph. I've never even met this mysterious Ashley. When are you going to have her over?"

"For a play date?" I said. "We're a little old for that."

"I'd like to meet her. I don't care that she's gay, you know."

I stared at her, wondering how she even knew that.

"I'm not stupid, Jazzie. I catch on. I read between the lines. And while I may not understand the whole homosexuality thing, I certainly appreciate that it is a reality. I'm a pretty flexible old woman, in case you hadn't noticed."

I held in a laugh and managed to keep a straight face. "Well, I didn't think you'd care. She's a competitive swimmer, and she's really good, so she spends most of her time in the pool. Which is why she doesn't come over, not because I didn't think you couldn't handle it."

Grandma harrumphed at me. "She swims? I wish you'd swim. I never understood why you gave swimming up. You know, your grandfather overruled me on that one, but I've always regretted not putting you in more lessons. What if you fall off a boat?"

"When's the last time I was on a boat?"

Grandma cleared her throat. "You never know when life will invite you on a boat."

"Really, Grandma? I've made it this far without an invite."

"Well, that's because your grandfather was as afraid of the water as you were. All the more reason to get you swimming. I might want to take you on a cruise or something, except I can't because you don't swim."

"You would never go on a cruise," I told her. "You're too busy."

"Well, someday I might want to." She harrumphed again. "Your grandpa was stubborn. Just like you. He didn't want to make you feel bad about fearing water. I thought you should overcome it. I should have put my foot down."

She cleared her throat and glanced at the watch on her thin wrist. "Why don't you bring Ashley over after work if she's not swimming? I'd like to meet her."

"I'm meeting Mom after work to go shopping."

"You are?" She frowned and sat down on the end of my bed. "Can you do me a favor? She's really not dealing with her last trimester well. Poor Simon."

I reached for my charm and rolled it in my fingers. "Poor Simon? He's the one who got her pregnant."

"Your mom's acting very temperamental." Grandma's expression looked as sour as it did when she drank her daily green-vegetable supplement. She'd tried to make me take that stuff, but it tasted truly horrible. I made such a big deal about gagging that she gave up on trying to force me.

"She's put on a ton of weight, and she can't walk without waddling. Plus, it's been raining around here for weeks. Who wouldn't be grouchy?"

Grandma stood and went to my dresser. "I think it's more than that. She's upset all the time. Pregnancy isn't supposed to be so, I don't know, hard. She wasn't like this with you. Maybe it's because she's older? I hope she and Simon aren't having problems."

She picked up my framed picture of Grandpa from my dresser, smiled at it, and put it down. "Anyhow. Would you do me a favor and talk to her? You know your mom. She won't listen to me. You're better with her about stuff like this."

"I am?"

Grandma nodded. "Yes. She listens to you. You know she isn't always very secure about herself. She's had to make some tough decisions in her life, hold her head high while people criticized her."

Including her own mother, I wanted to add. Grandma was hard on her sometimes. She didn't let Mom forget she was the one who raised me.

"Try to get her out of her bad mood," Grandma told me, as if I had a magic wand I could wave that would cheer up my mom instantly.

"Maybe take her some of those fresh homemade chocolate cookies from Grinds. She loves those. She needs to cheer up for the baby."

Grandma reached into her sweater pocket and pulled out a twenty-dollar bill.

"Buy us some treats too, if you want." She handed me the money.

I shoved it in my jean pocket, wishing twenty dollars would buy Mom a new boyfriend. Now, that'd be a real treat.

• • •

After my shift, I hurried into Amber's office at the back of the coffee shop.

"Hi, Amber."

She glanced up from the schedule on the computer screen in front of her. "Hmm?"

"Um. Would it be okay if I took Wednesdays off for a while?"

Amber chewed the pen lid in her mouth, staring at the spreadsheet in front of her. "It's not a busy night. Shouldn't be a problem. What's up?" She looked up at me for a second and then glanced back to her screen.

"My grandma wants me to volunteer at the church."

Amber tore her eyes away from the computer screen. "Church?" She grinned.

"As a musician-slash-helper for the seniors. Sort of like karaoke night. I'll play guitar."

Amber laughed. "Really? That's awesome."

I shrugged. "Grandma always gets me into stuff like that." I thought about what Mom had said. "I think she wants to save the world."

"From what?"

"I don't know. Good music?" I smiled. "She thinks everyone should join in her efforts."

"Well, good for her. And good for you for pitching in. I'll pull you off Wednesdays." She typed something on her keyboard. "Oh. Lacey's booked a few off too. Oh, well. No problem. Jackson and I can handle it. It's not busy."

"Thanks." I turned to go.

"Hey, Jaz."

I glanced over my shoulder. "Yup?"

"Is everything okay with you and Lacey?" Amber scratched at her short red hair.

I lifted my shoulder and turned back to face her.

"Does it have anything to do with whatever happened between you and Nathan?"

"No. I mean, there is no me and Nathan." I hadn't seen him much lately, and when I did, he ignored me.

Amber tilted her head, watching me, and then grinned mischievously. "What about Jackson? You two have a good time working together."

My face warmed. "We're just friends."

Amber lifted her pen to her mouth again and chewed the end. "You sure you don't have a little thing for him?"

"Me? No. No way." I was horrified. Did it show?

Amber laughed. "Don't look so mortified. He's a good guy. Cute."

I didn't dignify her with an answer. I wondered if she knew he might be dealing again. I didn't have any real proof, just the odd phone calls he got and how he turned his back on me when he took them.

"Okay. Never mind. What do I know? I'm just your boss, right?"

"Exactly." I made a mental note to tone it down around Jackson at work. I didn't want to give anyone the wrong impression. I had no desire to make people think we were anything but friends.

I left her office and went around the corner, almost smacking right into Lacey. We did an awkward dance, moving to the same side and then back again until Lacey grabbed my arm.

"Hey, long time, no talk." She beamed at me like a long-lost friend, which I guess she was. "I just came by for a coffee. I was about to go in to say hey to Amber." She paused. "You want to sit down and have something to drink?"

"I can't." I didn't say anything about meeting my mom for shopping. Before the Simon episode, I'd have invited Lacey along, but now I had no desire to see Mom and Lacey chatting and laughing together about anything.

Lacey blinked. "I guess you're still mad at me."

"No." A total lie.

"We haven't hung out in ages." She pushed out her bottom lip.

"I see you at work."

"I know. But we haven't hung out." She paused for a moment, tugging at the bottom of her shirt. "I miss you."

I lifted a shoulder and avoided her eyes. What did she expect from me?

"I'm not stupid, Jaz. I know what I did was wrong."

I shifted from one foot to the other. It was the perfect chance to ask the question I was afraid of asking. How far she and Simon had gone? I was afraid she didn't remember. Afraid that she did.

"Are you avoiding me because of Nathan?" she asked.

I shook my head and wanted to shake her. "Nathan doesn't even talk to me anymore."

"Well, you blew him off. You should have let him cut the cord. Guys need to do that. It saves face, especially after hooking up."

"I guess I don't have your experience. And we didn't hook up. Not really."

"That right? That's not what Nathan said." Lacey shifted from one hip to the other. Bada boom, bada bing.

"I didn't sleep with him, and you know it."

"Do I?" She twirled hair around her finger. Around and around. "You fooling around with Jackson now?"

Blood rushed to my cheeks. "We're friends."

Lacey flipped her blond hair with her hand. "Well, try not to fool around with Jackson. It'll ruin another friendship." She glared at me. "It seems like you're running out. Next you'll lose the lesbian, and I imagine she's hard to get rid of."

Lacey spun on her heels and stomped away from me in a huff. Her words hung in the air, but I couldn't let them just dangle there. I took off after her, following her out to the parking lot. I caught up to her and grabbed her by the shoulder.

"You've never even bothered to get to know Ashley," I told her. "And thanks for believing Nathan over me. I don't care what he said. It's not true. I'm nothing like you."

She glared at me. "Meaning what?"

"I'm not a slut."

She blinked quickly, and we stared at each other in shock. I didn't know which one of us was more surprised by what I'd said to her.

A car honked behind me, demanding us to move out of the way. Lacey lifted her middle finger and the driver drove around us, screeching and squealing away.

Her eyes shone. "You know, you're the one person who never made me feel like that was true," she said. "You are the only person who didn't think of me like that."

"Like what?" I demanded, wanting her to say it. Admit what she was.

"A slut," she whispered.

"Well, I guess things change."

Lacey opened her mouth to speak but I kept going.

"Nathan is the first person I've even made out with. And yes, I was drunk, but it was horrible. I would never keep doing that. I hated myself for it. And I didn't have sex with him. I stopped before we went too far. I shouldn't even have to tell you that." I growled in frustration. I sounded like her. Defensive. But this wasn't about me. "But even if I did, even if we had, Nathan doesn't have a girlfriend, so what would it matter?"

We eyed each other warily, like two gunfighters with our hands on our holsters.

"Why Simon, Lacey? Do you need to go after all the taken ones too? Couldn't you leave one guy on the planet alone?"

Lacey's head dropped to her chest after I pulled the first trigger.

"I don't even remember much," she said softly. "I don't remember how it happened. I just remember looking up and seeing you." She lifted her head with pleading eyes staring at me. "Your face. The way you were looking at me."

I hardened my heart against the tears that plopped down her cheeks. "This time I can't just forgive you," I told her.

"You can't forgive me?" Lacey said. "I don't forgive myself, Jaz. I feel awful. I wish I could take it back, but I can't."

I hardened my heart. "No, you can't."

She wiped her nose with the back of her hand and rubbed under her eyes with her fingertip.

Her misery hurt me. "Why, Lacey? Why do you have to be this way?" I asked.

Her lips pressed together tight. "You want to know?" she asked and blew out a puff of air. Her voice turned icy. "You want to know the truth?" Her voice cracked with emotion. "Remember how I told you about my stepfather? Number two. The way he watched me. Trying to sneak in when I showered or changed?"

I squirmed and bit my lip, nodding.

"Well, what I didn't tell you, what I forgot to mention was that number one was worse. Much worse."

I swallowed a lump of dread. "What do you mean?"

"I think you know what I mean." Her voice was bitter, dripping with cold. "He did more than watch. The only person I ever told was my mom, and you know what she did? She blamed it on me. She said that I asked for it." Lacey closed her eyes for a moment and took a deep breath. When she opened them, her eyes were full of hate. "I was only thirteen. A kid. What kid asks for that?"

I swore softly under my breath, but she kept going.

"Mom dumped him, but before long she brought home number two. At least number two only looked. I had to live with that until I was old enough to get out of there."

Another car pulled into the parking lot, its wheels crunching over the pavement, but it pulled into a spot behind Lacey, and neither one of us moved.

"So maybe that's why I drink. To try to forget. It doesn't take a psychology degree to figure it out. Why I'm such a slut, as you said."

I opened my mouth to speak and closed it. I tried again. "I'm sorry, Lacey. I mean, why didn't you tell me before?"

She stepped back, looking away from me. "Because I didn't have to, Jaz. I don't go around bragging about the gory details in my life. You accept me for who I am. Or you did. You put up with my stupid drinking. And the boys. You never made me feel like I was a bad person because of it. Until now."

A third car pulled into the parking lot and stopped, waiting for us to move. Lacey stared at me, her expression wounded but at the same time just as hateful as mine felt. The car honked and I walked off to the side. Lacey didn't move. She seemed to be waiting for me to say something.

"I'm sorry that happened to you," I managed, but my voice was strained. I wanted to go to her, take her by the hand, and move her out of the way, but I couldn't.

Why had we never told each other the secrets we carried around? Talked about the things that had happened to us? We'd been drawn together, sensing somehow our wounds and differences, but we'd never opened up. We'd never talked about the things that could have brought us closer. Maybe we could have helped each other sooner.

The driver in the car rolled down his window. "Hey, would you get out of the way already?"

"Forget it, Jaz. Just forget everything." Lacey started to run. Her feet pounded on the ground. I felt paralyzed, stuck to the cement and helpless as I watched her go, unable to go after her and give her what she needed from me. I couldn't forgive her. No matter what had happened to her in the past.

My insides gurgled with bile. My stomach churned with my inability to forgive my best friend. Or Simon. I couldn't forgive either of them for what they'd done.

• • •

I walked down the busy hallway in the mall, spotting Mom at our meeting place in front of the food court. I hurried toward her, clutching the paper bag full of cookies I'd brought from work.

She whimpered when she saw the bag. "Oh, God. No. Not the cookies. Take them away. Please." She stepped back to distance herself from the bag. "I don't need cookies around me right now. Willpower. Zero."

I dropped my arm, shifting the bag to my other hand.

"I'm such a cliché, aren't I? Fat pregnant woman with raging hormones." She started waddling away with a crazy look in her eyes. "I want to buy you some new clothes. Thin clothes. Live vicariously through you. You, skinny minny, got your metabolism from someone else."

"You mean the Sperminator?"

She clucked her tongue on the roof of her mouth just like Grandma and lifted a shoulder. Him again, her expression said. She'd brought him up, not me.

"Maybe." She stopped. "Anyways. Here. Let's go in here."

She grabbed my arm and dragged me into a trendy jean store. "Pick out any pair of jeans. What are you, size four?"

"Um. Two," I answered, embarrassed at my skinniness. I headed for the jean rack, my enthusiasm for a new pair of jeans dampened by the mention of the Sperminator.

Mom groaned, shuffling behind me. "My thigh is a size two right now. Why don't you try some different styles? You have such a cute figure." She sounded almost annoyed.

I made a face and flicked through a rack of jeans. She always tried to get me to wear what she liked.

"Jaz?"

"Mmm?" I studied jean styles without enthusiasm.

"Do you think Simon really loves me?"

I stopped flipping past pant styles. "What? Of course, he loves you," I lied.

Did a man who loved his pregnant girlfriend make out with her daughter's best friend? If yes, he was head over heels.

"I'm worried Simon won't be able to handle fatherhood. His dad couldn't. He fooled around on his mom until they divorced." She laughed, but her humor quickly dissolved and her face crumpled. Fine lines deepened around her eyes. "I don't know what's wrong with me these days. I'm mad at everyone. I want to kill Simon.

Your grandma is making me crazy. I spend every day at work trying not to yell at my customers or cry." Tears plopped down her cheeks. "Can I have the cookies?"

Flustered, I handed the bag to her.

A salesclerk appeared out of nowhere, a sneering teenage girl about my age with curly auburn hair piled on top of her head. She clacked on gum and shook her head. "No food in the store, ladies."

Ignoring her, Mom pulled a cookie out of the bag and bit off a big hunk. Crumbs fell to the carpet. "My doctor tells me I'm gaining too much weight, but all I want to do is eat." She shoved the entire cookie in her mouth and chewed.

"Hey, no eating in the store."

I shot the girl an evil eye and put a hand on Mom's back, pushing her toward the exit of the store. "You're not fat. You're pregnant," I said to calm her.

"Ha. I'm as big as a house." She sniffled and handed the bag back. "Take it away from me." She patted her stomach. "I'm supposed to be glowing and beautiful. Instead I'm huge. And grouchy. With pimples." She sniffled again. "Don't let Grandma throw me a baby shower, okay? I can't handle a party."

"I'll try." I tried to think of something reassuring to say. "Anyway, you look great. You're supposed to have weird cravings and be grouchy, aren't you? Maybe you're just tired. You should sleep more. Let's go. I don't need a new pair of jeans, anyway."

She just stood there with a sad expression.

"Really, Mom. I don't."

She flashed a fake smile. "Sorry, Jaz. I didn't mean to wreck our shopping trip. Listen to me rattling on about myself." She wiped cookie crumbs off the side of her lip. "I'll take you shopping after the baby is born. I promise. We'll have lots of time to spend together doing fun things. Like shopping."

She reached inside her purse and pulled out keys. "I'll drive you home." She sniffled loudly. "Sorry. I'm up and down like a roller coaster on speed, but I'm fine." She held out her hand. "Give me the rest of those cookies."

I handed her the bag without a word.

"To hell with calories. I've been on a diet my whole life. I'm pregnant, and I'm letting loose."

As we headed for the exit, I watched her uncharacteristically gobble a handful of cookies. Her bloated face looked miserable.

"Simon loves you. He'll be there for this baby," I said. I felt worse telling another giant lie but she ate it up, just like the cookies.

chapter ten

At least school was a place that offered solitude. No mom weeping about her size or discomfort. No grandma telling me to get out of my room, off my guitar, and out in the fresh air. And with my grades still hanging in there, teachers left me alone. When my schedule didn't jibe with Ashley's, my favorite place between classes was outside. Alone in the unseasonable warmth with my guitar, I closed my eyes and faintly hummed the lyrics of my latest song.

Betray me. Betray you. I will if I must.

"What's that?" a voice asked.

My body jerked, and my eyes flew open as a gasp escaped my mouth.

"Sorry. Didn't mean to scare you. Is it okay if I sit here?" Jackson said nonchalantly, as if he came and sat with me at school every day. Which he didn't. Ours was mostly a coffee-shop thing.

"It's a free country." I sat up, not wanting him to see that his proximity made my nerves jump around like toddlers overdosing on sugar.

"Yeah, I hear it is," he said as he plunked down on the grass beside me. He switched his iPod off, pulling earbuds from his ears and letting the wires dangle in front of his shirt.

"So you realize you're sitting outside the school all by yourself, strumming and humming?" he asked in a conversational tone.

"I do indeed." I crunched my legs and hugged myself tighter.

"Perhaps this is one of the reasons you're considered a freak by some of our esteemed classmates." He winked to take the edge off.

"Perhaps." Resting my chin on the top of my knobby knees, I studied him. "But an advantage of people thinking I'm a freak is freedom to act like one. No one thinks anything of it."

"I see your point. Unexpected privileges. So. What song were you playing?"

"It's just a song."

"I don't recognize it."

"I guess not." I held my breath a little as if I was about to tell him I wasn't wearing underwear or something. "I wrote it."

"You wrote it?"

I nodded, waiting for his reaction and realizing it mattered.

"Cool." He grinned at me like I'd done something amazingly clever. A better reaction than I'd hoped for.

"You crack me up, you know," he said. "Putting yourself out there with some things and trying to just blend into the scenery and not be noticed with others."

"What makes you think you know so much about me?"

"I'm good at figuring people out. It's a gift."

"That right?" I asked.

"I know you work in a coffee shop but hate drinking coffee. I know that you're obsessed with Neil Diamond, and I know you're kind of a lone wolf. But how come I didn't know that you wrote a song?" He leaned back, his hands pressing into the grass, and watched me.

"Songs," I admitted. "I've been writing songs for years."

He pushed off the grass and wiped his hands back and forth on each other. "Plural. You're prolific. I guess I should have known."

My insides smiled at his easy teasing. He was so much easier to talk to now.

"What's it about?"

The shine inside me dimmed, and I shrugged and glanced around us at the front of the school yard. "It's kind of private." The song and the content. I couldn't tell him the inspiration for my bitter ballad. Seeing Simon and Lacey.

Jackson picked a long blade of grass and stuck the end in his mouth and chewed on it. "That right? You still keeping secrets from me?"

I studied the grass in his lips, wondering why he was chomping on the lawn but feeling envious of the blade nonetheless. I frowned at myself.

"Hey, cheer up. They can't be that bad."

I slowly breathed out and shrugged, pretending nonchalance.

"That's cool. I mean, that you write songs. I'm quite the singer myself." He grinned at me and I smiled. He sang while we were working at the coffee shop. His voice wasn't bad but he always goofed around, exaggerating high notes and wiggling his hips.

"That song sounded kind of sad. Don't tell me…let me guess. It's about your one true love?" He grinned like a kid eager to share a silly knock-knock joke.

I stuck out my tongue. "If I ever write a song about true love, please shoot me."

"Why?" he asked.

"Because it doesn't exist."

Jackson tilted his head. "You don't really believe that, do you?"

"I've never seen it." I'd thought my mom and Simon were in love like that. But look what he'd done to her. And true, Grandpa Joe and Grandma had been married for a million years, but it's not like they were big on public displays of affection. Never mind that demonstrations of passion from my grandparents would have grossed me out anyhow. I couldn't remember ever seeing them kiss or hold hands. Grandma was very proper.

"Maybe you will. One day. Maybe it will even happen to you."

I studied the lawn to cover up the flutters in my belly, then picked a blade of grass and stuck it in the corner of my mouth the way he was doing. "My song isn't about love. Kind of the opposite, really. It's more about a secret that could destroy love, actually. A secret that can never be told."

He tilted his head. "Intriguing. Is it based on fact?"

I shrugged, excited to share a tiny bit of what I'd been holding inside for months. "I have to protect someone else."

He curled up his lip in a sexy half grin, tugging on the grass hanging out of the corner of his mouth. "You know, Jaz. I told you I'm good at keeping secrets if you need to talk. I have a few of my own. We could do a swap. Kind of like exchanging blood. Only less painful. And more sanitary."

I wanted to know his secrets so badly that I bit the blade in half to keep from asking. I tasted grass and spit it out and then shook my head.

"Well, keep it in mind. The deal stands." He sat up straighter. "You working tonight?"

"Nope." I tried not to show disappointment at the topic change. I wanted to know more about what he hid from the world. Like maybe his dealing? I wanted to ask him if he still did it. I wanted to tell him to stop. That it worried me.

"Too bad," he said.

My heart pattered a little more. I studied his features. His slightly crooked, thin nose. I wondered if he'd broken it. Maybe at juvie? I didn't want him to go back there or, worse, to jail.

"I don't work Wednesdays," I told him instead of begging him to stay out of trouble. "My grandma signed me up to do volunteer work."

"That right?"

I nodded.

"I totally see you as the volunteer type. Candy striper? Short little skirt with extra-high heels?" He grinned at the preposterous image.

I burst out laughing. "Not quite."

"So what are you doing then? Feeding the hungry? Saving the environment?"

"Jaz?" A voice interrupted us.

We both turned. Ashley stood close by. She was staring down at us, her eyebrows raised slightly. I'd been so wrapped up in my conversation with Jackson that I hadn't even heard her approach.

She smiled. Today her hair tips were dyed neon yellow. She adjusted her glasses and lifted her hand in greeting.

"Hey, Ashley," I said. "You know Jackson, right?"

Ashley lifted her hand again. "I know who he is, but we don't have classes together. We've never officially met. You work with Jaz, right?"

"You mean she doesn't talk about me? I'm crushed." Jackson grinned at her playfully. "So you're the famous lesbian of the school."

"And you're the juvenile delinquent," Ashley shot back.

"Touché," he said and tilted an invisible hat.

I stood, wiping grass from my butt. "I can't believe you two haven't met before."

"I don't take women's studies." Jackson grabbed my hand and used it to pull himself up.

"I don't study criminology," Ashley said.

I laughed. "Come on. Let's go inside. It's almost time for class." Jackson let go of my hand, and I secretly wished he'd hold it all the way inside the school.

I hurried forward in case he'd read my thoughts, and Jackson and Ashley quickly caught up. The three of us headed toward the school as a group, with Jackson in the middle. It felt nice, like I had people.

When we reached the front door, Jackson opened it and held it for Ashley and me. "You have classes this afternoon?" he asked.

"Chemistry and math," I told him.

"I've got a free period," he said. "How sweet is that?"

"Me too," Ashley told him. "I'd hang with you, but you don't seem to like lesbians." The corner of her mouth twitched up. She glanced at me, something unreadable but nice in her eyes.

"You heard wrong. I happen to highly approve of lesbians." He raised his eyebrows suggestively.

"It's not a spectator sport, you know." She smacked him on the arm.

Jackson laughed his kooky baritone laugh. I poked his other arm, trying not to notice how solid it was. I had an urge to touch it again for reference. "Jerk!"

He bowed his head with a smile. "I jest. I'm off. See you later, ladies." He headed off into the loud hallway and away from us. I stopped to watch him go.

"Hey," Ashley said, pushing her shoulder against mine. "You're staring at the pretty boy like he's a big old scoop of vanilla ice cream."

I stopped staring and smacked Ashley back. "I am not. And since when do you think boys are pretty?"

"Um. You were so. And I'm gay, Jaz. Not blind. He's hot. And he seems cool. I don't know why you've been keeping him to yourself. I'm glad you finally introduced me."

"I haven't been keeping him to myself…we just usually don't hang out at school. And you never come to Grinds."

"Yeah, because I'm in the pool. And since you and Lacey had your mysterious fight, you're never at Marnie's anymore either." She glanced down the hallway. "Maybe if Marnie feels comfortable, we could double-date." She looked at me and started laughing. "Chill. I'm only teasing you. Ha. You should see your face!"

I narrowed my eyes and gave her a dirty look, not amused.

We came to a "T" in the hallway and Ashley pointed left. "I'm this way. You want to meet on the front steps at lunch?"

"Sure." I waved and rushed to my own class, cheered by an unusual sense of belonging.

• • •

I met up with Ashley at my locker, and we grabbed our lunch bags and then headed for some fresh air outside. This time of day, kids would be sprawled all over the front walk and steps, spilling onto the lawn and enjoying the break from class.

As soon as I stepped outside, the sunlight blinded me. I breathed in cool, fresh air and heard a car horn honking. Just another car alarm going off, I assumed. I assumed wrong.

"Jaz. Hey, Jaz," a voice shouted over the noise.

I lifted my hand to block the sun and tensed when I spotted the person shouting.

"What the heck is he doing here?"

"Hey. That's Simon," Ashley said, noticing him at the same time.

"No kidding." I swore under my breath and snarled. "What does he want?"

Simon waved his arms in the air and jumped up and down on the other side of the road.

"Hey, Jaz! Jaz," he shouted.

He seemed reluctant to cross the sidewalk separating the school yard from the road, even though in jeans and a T-shirt and hoodie he barely looked older than most of the high-school kids. I wanted to yell at him to get away from the school. Get away from me.

People stared, watching him and then me. I spotted Tina and her clones a few feet away. Tina was standing and looking around as if she was waiting for someone.

"Another new boyfriend?" Tina called when she saw me.

"It can't be. She's with the lesbian," one of Tina's groupies squealed.

"I liked it better when they ignored me," I said.

Ashley raised her middle finger without looking over.

Simon continued waving his arms. I lifted my hand to let him know I'd seen him and to stop his ridiculous gesturing. "I have to go see what he wants," I told Ashley, even though he was the last person in the world I wanted to talk to. "Do you mind? I'll catch up with you later, okay?"

"Uh, I guess not," Ashley said. "Things cool between you guys now?"

I ignored her and hurried down the sidewalk toward Simon, eager to get away from the people watching us. I hurried to cross the road, but when I reached him, I stopped.

"What?" I demanded, frowning at his expensive designer sunglasses. Who was he trying to impress?

He grinned. "Hey. I haven't seen you in ages, and that's all I get? What?"

I clutched my lunch bag close. "What are you doing here, Simon? You're a little too old to be hanging around my high school."

His sunglasses almost hid his hurt expression. Almost. He smiled again with regular voltage. "I knew you'd come outside for your lunch break. I'm on a break from work too. We're doing a house close by, so I thought I'd pop over to see if I could take you for lunch."

I uncrossed my arms and lifted my brown paper bag in the air. "I brought lunch. Grandma insists I don't waste my money."

He stepped toward me and took the bag out of my hand. "Throw it out. I'll buy you something hot and greasy."

I glanced behind me at the school. Ashley had disappeared. "Grandma will be pissed if I throw out my lunch."

"Don't tell her. You don't need to tell her everything you do, you know."

I already knew Simon was good at hiding things.

"Come on, Jaz." He pushed the bag toward me. "Save it for later if you don't want to throw it out. I'll buy you McD's." He put an arm on my shoulder. "I'd really like to talk to you. It's been awhile." He squeezed my shoulder. "It's important."

I wanted to say no. I pressed my lips tighter.

"Please."

I grabbed my bag from his hand and wiggled my shoulder away from him.

He pointed to his car. His stupid yellow Beetle. "Come on. I'm parked illegally."

We were being watched. I had a couple of choices. Make a big scene and stomp away. Or, go and deal with him in private.

"Fine." I strutted to the passenger door, yanked on the handle, pulled the door open, and jumped inside.

I tossed my paper bag into the backseat as Simon climbed into the driver's seat. He started the engine without noticing. I hoped my lunch would rot and smell up his car.

"Thanks for coming," he said. "I'll make it a fast lunch and have you back in time for your next class, I promise."

"Whatever." I pulled down the strap on my seat belt, buckling myself in and crossing my arms as he pulled away from the curb. Tina stared at us from the school yard as we drove away.

He drove past the high school and turned right at the light instead of left.

"McDonald's is the other way," I told him.

"I know. I thought we'd go to the one at the mall. The one by the high school's always so packed. Especially at noon."

"I have a class at one."

"I said I'll have you back on time. Don't worry." He sounded pissed off and drove for a moment before saying anything else. "So. How's school?" he asked, like it was an effort to be friendly.

"It's fine." I reached for the volume knob on his stereo and cranked up the music, even though it was a CD of stupid hip-hop songs I couldn't stand.

He bobbed his head to the music, not even appreciating my intentional rudeness.

When we got to the mall, we went to the food court. Simon pointed to an open table and told me to save us seats. He headed to a line to order for us, and I stomped to the empty table and sat waiting for him, wanting to take off and leave him all alone.

A few minutes later he joined me, carrying a plastic tray covered with fast food.

"Big Mac, large fries, large Coke?" he said, unloading the food from the tray. My standard order.

"You should have asked before you ordered for me," I snapped, just to be disagreeable.

"Oh." He looked upset. "Sorry. I just assumed since that's what you always get. I got a Chicken Grill. You can have mine if you want."

My fingers reached for the burger. "It's okay," I mumbled, feeling silly. "I don't want to wreck your diet. I know older guys like you need to watch what they eat."

He eyeballed his chicken sandwich and unwrapped it, ignoring my dig. "So, I'm worried about your mom. I thought you might be able to help."

The burger that hovered in my hand, poised for a bite, lost all its appeal. I dropped it in the wrapper on my tray. My appetite vanished for good.

"Why are you worried about my mom?"

His eyebrows pressed together, and apprehension radiated from his dark skin. I had a vivid image of him pressing up against Lacey and wanted to reach across the table to smack him. Hard. To leave an imprint on that skin.

"She's. Well, she's acting really…" He struggled for a word. "Odd."

"She's really pregnant," I said. Did he really need to be reminded?

"I know. But it's more than that. I don't know what to do. She doesn't seem happy with me. With anything, really. And she's angry. Really angry. All the time. Man, I wish my mom was alive. I'd ask her these questions."

I wished Simon's mom was still alive too. Stupid cancer. I couldn't stand his wounded expression. I looked over at the table beside us. Girls younger than me giggled and flirted with a nearby table of boys. Middle-school kids probably skipping class. I envied them.

"What do you expect me to do?" I asked, still watching the kids.

"I don't know. Nobody knows her as well as you do. I thought maybe she said something to you when you went shopping. About why she's so unhappy."

My eyes narrowed. "She's pregnant, Simon. She has raging hormones, and she's gaining weight. You know how she is about her looks. It's probably normal for her to act grumpy."

His shoulders drooped, and he ran a hand through his tight black curls. "I don't know. I've talked to a couple of other guys with kids, and they said their wives were fine. I mean, moody and kooky when they were pregnant, but not like her. She's more…I don't think she's supposed to be like this."

"So? Are you asking for my permission to walk out on her? Because she's not acting the way you think a pregnant woman should act?"

His expression changed. He looked almost offended. "I'm not leaving her. I'm worried about her."

Raw emotion crept into his features, making him look older and troubled. There were new wrinkles under his eyes and bags, as if he hadn't been sleeping well. And his cheeks were drawn, thinner.

For an instant I felt sorry for him, the old Simon, the one I used to get along with. I remembered how he used to make me laugh. And the serious talks we'd had too. I stared at the table, remembering once when we'd been goofing around in the living room at home. Mom was in the kitchen trying to help Grandma make dinner.

He had pressed his arm up beside mine.

"We're almost the same shade," he'd said.

I'd bit my lip shyly and nodded. "I don't know anyone else like me," I told him.

"There's lots of people like you. Maybe not in Tadita but in other places. Lots, so don't you forget it."

I looked up at Simon. At his warm, caring eyes. He'd helped me, made me feel less alone.

And then the other memory flashed in my mind. The sight of him devouring Lacey. It made me feel sick. I glared at him, full of hate.

He deserved to be miserable. Maybe it was karma. Payback. I shrugged and took a bite of my hamburger, even though chewing it gave me as much joy as gnawing on leather. I choked down a mouthful.

"What do I know? I'm seventeen. I don't know how pregnant women act." I picked up my drink and slurped.

Simon shifted on his chair.

I wanted to add that I didn't know how expectant fathers acted either, but making out with younger women probably wasn't exactly normal.

He picked up his chicken sandwich but didn't bite into it. "God. I'm a jerk. I forget sometimes how you must feel about your dad. I, of all people, should get the dad thing." He pasted a grown-up, understanding expression on his face. "When my dad left us to go to England, I felt completely abandoned. Like yesterday's trash. Like it was my fault somehow that he would take off to another country and choose not to see his sons."

He put the chicken sandwich back down. "It's too heavy. I shouldn't have come to you with this. It's fine. Your mom is fine." He picked up his lunch, ripped off part of his sandwich with his teeth, and chomped.

"Simon," I told him slowly. "This has nothing to do with my dad or lack of. Trust me. And I really don't know how she's supposed to behave. She's having a baby."

"I know. Forget it. It's fine. She's just pregnant. I'm being stupid." He sucked on his straw, drinking his Diet Coke. "I'm not leaving," he added. "In case you're worried. I love her. I'm not going anywhere."

I swallowed another bite of hamburger. It tasted like lumpy clay and hurt going down. I wanted to spit out the truth, to tell him what I'd seen. Him. With Lacey. I wanted to scream. Purge the ugliness from inside me. I opened my mouth.

"So. How's song writing?" Simon asked in a lighter tone, obviously trying to move on to a safer topic. "Written anything new?"

I held my breath, trying to force myself to tell him what I had seen. I opened my mouth and then closed it, hating myself. I wanted to tell him what I thought of it, of him. But I couldn't do it. Instead, I just nodded.

"What's the song about?" He reached across the tray and grabbed a handful of my fries, shoving them into his mouth. He wasn't as cool as he pretended to be. Mom said he only ate fattening food when something was bothering him.

I pushed the rest of the fries toward him. "Have them. I'm not hungry." I hoped he'd gain 20 pounds. In his gut. And lose all his hair.

"Well?" he asked.

"It's about betrayal. Inspired by things in my life." I dropped my burger for good. My fingers wrapped around my charm bracelet, and I tried to calm myself.

Simon shoveled fries into his mouth, still watching me. "Who betrayed you?" he asked. His frenzied chewing stopped.

"No one. It's nothing. Just teen stuff."

"You can talk to me." He smiled without showing teeth. "We're almost related, right? I'd like to help."

Beside me, one of the young girls snickered at something.

"No. You can't," I told him.

Simon leaned forward, his broad smile mocking the rage inside of me. "Of course I can. Some of us guys are good ones. Let's face it. You're stuck with me now."

Anger flushed my cheeks. Stuck with him and keeping his secret. I started to stand and Simon reached for me. Almost in slow motion, as if on its own accord, my hand lifted. Simon's smile turned into a puzzled frown. Then a loud bang like a gun being fired filled the air. My hand smacked against his flesh.

"Jaz, what's wrong with you?"

An old woman standing behind Simon gasped, but for a second I saw a flash of satisfaction in her eye. Simon's face registered shock, hurt, and disbelief.

We stared at each other, and then I spun around. My arm caught the corner of our tray. Food clattered on the floor, and the sound of it mixed with amused giggles from people sitting around us.

I ran. I raced out into the mall, afraid he'd be on my heels. When it became obvious he wasn't, I stopped. I dug inside my jacket pocket and grabbed my cell. Dialed. It rang once.

"Hello?" said an impatient voice.

I glanced around. "Mom? It's me." Simon definitely wasn't following.

"Jaz? Are you okay? What's wrong?"

"Nothing's wrong. I was just, you know, thinking about you."

"That's sweet. But I'm at work and busy. Is there something important you need to talk to me about?" She sounded annoyed.

I paused. "Not really." Every fiber screamed at me to tell her. "I, um, wondered how you're doing. With the pregnancy and all."

"I'm uncomfortable as hell. If this baby even thinks about being late, I will reach up and yank it out of my body myself."

I made a face. "Mom. Gross."

She sighed. "Well, you asked. Did Simon ask you to call me? To see if I was okay?"

I didn't answer.

"Damn him. I told him not to."

So perceptive about some things and so oblivious about others.

"He didn't ask me to call. We kind of had a fight."

"Oh, Jaz. I really don't have time for this now." Mom sighed and lowered her voice. Her crisp, professional voice switched on. "Listen, honey. I'm about to see an important client. I have to go. Can we deal with this later?"

"Never mind." I paused. "It's nothing," I said. "I love you," I added softly, but she'd already hung up.

My fingers clutched the phone for a minute, and my eyes blinked fast to keep back the tears.

"Hey." A voice called, interrupting my thoughts.

I wiped under my eyes and looked up at the instantly recognizable voice. Nathan.

"What're you doing at the mall? Aren't you supposed to be in school?" He crossed his arms in front of himself.

I pushed a stray piece of hair behind my ear.

"Mmm. Check out that brown sugar," Nathan mumbled as a black girl with enormous hair extensions walked toward us. He didn't take his eyes off her butt as she strutted past. "No matter what else, you black girls have the nicest asses."

"Who said I was black?"

Nathan laughed and tore his eyes away from the girl's butt. "Look in the mirror."

I crossed my arms. "My mom's white."

Nathan shrugged. "So's Halle Berry's mom, but I don't see her denying her heritage. She's a proud black woman."

"Whatever." Debating skin color wasn't high on my to-do list.

"What're you doing here anyhow?" He grinned. "Looking for me?" His grin turned nasty.

My insides crawled. I whipped around and almost knocked over a girl standing behind me.

I froze. It was Tina. She snapped her gum, looking amused. She slipped past me and slid her arm through Nathan's. I wondered if she'd followed me there.

"Well, lookie here. A girl goes to the bathroom, and who sneaks over to try to steal my guy?" She smiled, but it wasn't friendly. "You're old news, Miss Thing."

My mouth opened, but nothing came out. I gaped at her, not moving or blinking.

"What happened to the hot old guy?" Tina asked and turned to Nathan. "She left school with some older black dude."

I didn't answer. Tina looked at Nathan. "She doesn't say much, does she?"

"That was probably Simon, her mom's boyfriend," Nathan said.

"Figures. Not like someone who's not gay or related is going to take her anywhere."

"Shut up." My hands clenched into fists.

Nathan snorted but looked away from me as if he was embarrassed.

"Oh. That's right. You do talk." Tina grinned and blew a big pink bubble and turned to Nathan. "Your ex here is after a drug dealer now, you know that?"

"That guy's a loser. Anyhow, I'm not into her." Nathan put an arm around Tina's shoulder and leaned over to slurp at her neck with his tongue. It made me want to vomit, but I couldn't stop staring at them, unable to move.

He glanced up from attacking her neck like it was dessert. "I guess I like my sugar white too."

"Much tastier," Tina added.

I regained control of my limbs and turned, but not before Tina shot me a triumphant look. She broke away from Nathan and leaned forward to whisper in my ear.

"Sorry about taking your man. Oh, wait. No, I'm not." She giggled. "Thought I'd see what all the fuss is about. You may be on to something. It is true what they say about black men, isn't it?"

I pushed her back and hurried toward the mall exit. My insides churned. Tina was with Nathan? I thought about taking a bus to Grinds and begging Lacey to tell me what she knew, but with a rush of heat to my face, I remembered. Lacey wasn't my friend anymore.

Instead of going to her, I climbed on the bus taking me back to school.

I said a silent prayer that the new romance between Tina and Nathan wouldn't cause me more problems. I didn't need help making my life any worse.

chapter eleven

Adjusting the guitar strap on my shoulder, I hurried up the front steps of the church and tiptoed down the hallway, a little nauseated by the stuffy air. It smelled like the trunk in Grandma's closet filled with Grandpa's old clothes and personal items. I headed to the kitchen and found Grandma sorting piles of packaged food on the long counter and talking to a girl about the same age as me. Grandma looked up and motioned me closer. I tried to tell by her expression if she'd heard about my fight with Simon or missing classes, but she merely seemed preoccupied.

"Jasmine, hi. This is Tanya. She's helping me put together food baskets."

I nodded at the girl, noticing her old clothes. No brand names on the jeans or plain blue sweatshirt. She smiled, friendly but cautious. I smiled back and sneaked another look at Grandma, breathing slower with relief.

From the back entrance, a pimply, tall boy walked into the kitchen, dangling a toddler in his arms.

"She needs her diaper changed, Tanya," he said with a squeamish grin and held the baby out.

Tanya put down a loaf of bread and hurried to the baby, cooing as she took her from the boy. She grabbed a diaper bag off the floor and disappeared around the corner toward the washrooms.

"If you can't handle that duty, Charlie, go bring in more groceries from the truck," Grandma ordered. "We've got twenty-five baskets to get out tonight, and the driver will be here in half an hour."

The boy grinned and nodded. "Deal." He headed back the way he'd come in.

Grandma shook her head and picked up the loaf of bread.

"That boy will not change diapers."

I didn't say anything.

"She's a good mom for such a young girl, and Charlie tries. They're good kids." She motioned me closer. "They volunteer almost every food-basket night."

I nodded. The girl would be about the same age as my mom when she had me. A couple of older kids marched into the kitchen carrying boxes of canned goods. Grandma rushed over, inspecting the boxes and pointing to the counter.

She looked over her shoulder. "Jasmine, your group is downstairs in the meeting room. Cede will help you out tonight, but after this week you'll have to handle the equipment yourself, so pay attention. Some of your group will use the karaoke machine, and some will want you to play guitar. You'll figure it out, right?"

I shifted the guitar on my shoulder. "Um. I guess. How many people?"

"Ten or twelve, I think. It's the bereavement group's social night. They voted for singing."

"Bereavement?" As in sad old people? Great.

"Most of them lost a spouse in the last year or so. Don't worry. They're not going to cry or demand therapy. They're here for fun." She opened a drawer and pulled out a sheet of paper.

"Here." She handed a sheet to Charlie. "Take this list and start putting together a box." She glanced over at me. "Cede's downstairs. She'll explain. Go. She's waiting."

I turned to leave, almost crashing into another girl who was walking into the kitchen with a stack of food in her arms. I blinked. It was Lacey.

"Hey. What's up? What're you doing here?" Lacey asked.

"Me? What about you?"

"Didn't I tell you Jasmine was helping out with karaoke night?" Grandma called to us. "I swear I lost my memory in the '90s." She gestured at Lacey. "Lacey's been helping me out with food baskets for the past couple months. But of course, you knew that."

"Uh. No."

Lacey put down her pile of food. "Don't look so surprised," she said.

Grandma groaned when Charlie knocked over a pile of canned goods. She raced away after a rolling can.

"I didn't know you were helping out my grandma," I said to Lacey.

"I guess that's because you've been so busy avoiding me," Lacey sniffed. "Anyway. I'm not doing it to impress you. Your grandma asked for my help. And I like it."

I nodded. I didn't want to feel sorry for her or forgive her for her tendency to go after inappropriate men. Like my mom's boyfriend, I reminded myself and headed for the exit.

"Jaz?" Lacey called as I started to leave.

I turned.

"You ever going to forgive me?" Lacey asked softly.

I glanced at Grandma, but she was busy piling up cans. I lifted my shoulder but didn't answer.

"How's your mom doing? I saw her the other day." Lacey glanced at Grandma, but she wasn't paying attention to us. "She wasn't very friendly."

I scowled. "She doesn't know," I whispered harshly. "She's having a hard time with her pregnancy, that's all."

Grandma looked up then and pointed at her watch.

"I gotta go," I told Lacey. "I'm doing karaoke downstairs."

Lacey's face loosened. "With the seniors?"

I nodded, a smile tugging at my lips. "Yup."

"Have fun with that, Spazzy."

Without thinking, I laughed out loud. A long time ago, Lacey and I promised each other we'd grow old together. Be roommates at an old folks' home. We'd called ourselves Spazzy and Looney and wreak havoc on the old men.

"I miss you, Spazzy," Lacey whispered. "You're my best friend."

My laughter disappeared. "I gotta go. See ya." I headed downstairs, wanting to get away from her and from the heaviness in my heart.

• • •

Karaoke went smoothly, but the sad voices of lonely seniors crawled under my skin. One old man reminded me so much of Grandpa that my heart ached. He asked me to play a Neil Diamond song on the guitar, and as he sang along, I had to bite my lip to keep from crying. I hurried out of the church when I was done, avoiding Grandma and Lacey.

I swung my guitar strap on my shoulder so it was comfortable and began to walk. I didn't think about where I was going or why. I just walked. Loneliness throbbed so badly inside that I struggled with my breathing. But I stared ahead and kept putting one foot in front of the other. Before I knew it, I was at Grinds.

I went inside. Behind the counter in the Pit, Jackson was spraying whipped cream onto a specialty coffee. He spotted me, and his smile warmed my insides. Instantly my impulse to come to see him seemed okay and not the stupidest idea I'd ever had. I hurried closer.

"I'm not stalking you," I said when I was close to him.

"Damn," he answered and placed the drink he'd finished making on the counter. "And here I was hoping."

A man in a suit gave me a dirty look and cut in front of me to grab the mug of steaming coffee. I stepped back, but I didn't take my eyes off Jackson. He was so handsome. So polite to the customers. The man grabbed his coffee and moved out of the way. I took a deep breath. It was now or never.

"Do you remember what you said about a rain check?" I asked.

Jackson nodded without hesitating. "Of course. No expiration date."

I let out a breath I didn't even realize I'd been holding, while clinging to my guitar for dear life.

"Well." I gnawed my lip. "I was wondering. If, well…when you get off, if I could, you know, take you up on it. I mean, could we talk?"

He glimpsed down at his wrist. "I'm off in fifteen. After that, I'm all yours."

I nodded, the combination of relief and nerves making speech temporarily impossible. For a minute I wished. Well, I wished that he really was all mine. Not just a friend.

But I needed a friend. I glanced around the coffee shop and then at the bookstore next door. "I'll come back. You're sure you're not too busy?"

"I'm sure." He grinned. "Hey, you were volunteering tonight, right?"

I bobbed my head up and down like a moron.

"How'd you get here?"

"I walked."

He stood on his tiptoes and peered over the counter at my feet. "Well, at least you had your shoes on this time."

I laughed, and more of my tension drained. It would be okay. I could talk to Jackson. Trust him. No matter what else, he was a good person. Inside. Where it counted.

I wandered over to the bookstore until Jackson's shift was over. When I returned, he was clocking out. He lifted his hand in a wave and motioned me over.

"You want to grab a seat in here?" Jackson asked from behind the counter.

"Um. Would you mind if we went somewhere else?"

Jackson didn't miss a beat. "You want to head over to Gracie's?" he asked. "They have awesome apple pie. I'm starving."

I nodded, my heart thumping. What if I told him the secret and everything went wrong? Could I really trust him?

chapter twelve

A tall, thin waiter seated us in a red leather booth at Gracie's. A few other couples were sitting at tables, but the atmosphere was quiet and intimate. Jackson waited while I tucked my guitar under the table, and then he slid in beside me. My leg accidentally pressed up against his. I moved it quickly, pretending not to notice the jolt. He didn't bat an eye. Without checking the dessert menu, he ordered a piece of apple pie. We both asked for sodas, and then the waiter disappeared.

"So. What's up?" Jackson asked.

I picked up a saltshaker, dumping a few grains on the table and running my finger over them as I tried to figure out what to say.

"You ever think you really know someone? But then you find out something horrible and it changes everything?"

Jackson leaned back against the leather. The red made his black hair shine.

"Not really," he answered. "Not much that people do surprises me anymore."

I glanced down at the salt grains before glancing up to meet his eyes. "I suck at reading people. Must be a genetic mutation. I have several."

Jackson blinked.

I bit down on my bottom lip. "I have a secret." I felt nervous, as if I was about to perform live without rehearsal, without memorizing the lyrics.

"Yeah. I kind of figured." Jackson winked and propped his arms along the back of the booth. I stared at the salt and drew a line in the sprinkles on the table. I tried to remember which shoulder to throw salt over to ward off bad luck. Superstition was a gift from Grandpa.

"You smiling about your secret?" Jackson asked.

"No." My lips quivered. "I wanted to throw salt over my shoulder to ward off bad luck, but I think it's too late."

I stopped playing with the salt. "It has to do with Lacey. Please don't repeat this, okay?"

He shook his head and his eyebrow rose. "Of course not."

"Lacey, well, she's had it tough. I guess she kind of deals with it by being with a lot of guys. She drinks too much. I've always figured it's kind of her way to cope, you know?"

Jackson nodded. "That's rough."

I looked around the restaurant, but no one was paying us the least bit of attention. "It is. I mean, I just wish she'd stop drinking so much. I hate when she lets guys…she's my best friend." I stopped and bit my lip again. "She was. She's not anymore."

Jackson nodded, and the waiter returned to our table and placed drinks in front of us. He smiled without speaking and quickly disappeared.

"I know that. So what happened?" Jackson asked when the waiter left.

I grabbed my straw and swirled the ice around, fizzing up the cola in my glass. I was afraid to say the truth out loud. I'd always protected Lacey. And my mom couldn't handle knowing. But I had to trust someone.

"I saw Lacey. With my mom's boyfriend, Simon. Making out."

Jackson whistled softly through his front teeth. "You're sure?"

"Definitely. In November. At Marnie's party. They were in the basement. I was looking for Lacey to tell her I was there. I didn't even know Simon was at the party. He'd come to pick up his brother, and, well, instead he picked up Lacey. I saw them. Very hot and heavy."

Jackson ran his fingers through his hair. "Whoa."

"I know. It's horrible, right? And the next day, when I was going to tell my mom the truth, I found out she was pregnant. So I couldn't tell her."

Jackson sipped his drink. "That's pretty harsh."

"I know." I shuddered, imagining them together, and then reached for the saltshaker, picked it up, and put it down again. "So anyhow. I belted him."

"What?"

"I did. Today. At lunch. I hit Simon in the face. He showed up at school and dragged me to McDonald's all hurt and upset that I wouldn't talk to him anymore. He was acting all worried about my mom, and I wanted to confront him, but I couldn't. Holding it in made me so angry that I smacked him."

Jackson tugged his bottom lip. "You are full of surprises." He studied me. "Did your mom find out? About him and Lacey?"

A tear slid out and rolled down my cheek. I wiped it away. "No, and I can't tell her. My grandma already says Mom isn't handling her pregnancy well. My grandma is worried about her. I mean, my mom's pretty old to be having another baby." I wiped under my eyes. "I haven't told anyone about Simon and Lacey. You can't tell a soul."

"I won't." He tugged on his bottom lip again. "Does he know you saw them?"

"No. Maybe he suspects now. But I doubt it. He thinks I'm being a jerk because I'm jealous that he's going to be around for my mom's baby."

"Man. That totally sucks. I'm really sorry, Jaz." Jackson picked up his drink and swallowed soda. He chewed on some ice thoughtfully. "So are you ever going to tell her?"

I thought about my mom and how she would probably have to leave Simon if she found out. She'd be left alone again. To raise her baby on her own. It wasn't what I wanted for her. I knew it wasn't what she wanted. Not again. I hesitated. "Do you think I should?"

"Man, it would mess things up."

I nodded once. "I know, right? How could she ever forgive him for doing that? Especially when she was pregnant. I mean, I wouldn't forgive that. Even if it was just kissing. It's still betrayal."

Jackson pulled his lip again, and I watched it pop back in place when he let go. I wondered if it was soft. If I'd ever know how it felt to kiss a boy like him. Not because I was drunk or because he had been dared to kiss me.

"It must have freaked him out, finding out about the baby. People do really stupid things when they're scared. And drunk."

"Not that stupid."

He nodded. "Has he done something like that before?"

"No. I mean, I don't think so. God. I don't know what to believe anymore. He seemed so in love with her. He still does." I reached out with my foot and nudged my guitar case. "Is this what guys do, Jackson? Get drunk and fool around?" I grabbed my guitar charm and rolled it between my fingers. "Do you think drinking makes it okay?"

"No, I don't."

His voice sounded uncertain though. I wondered if he'd ever done the same to some girl. My heart ached. For the girl and for me.

"He can't really love her though, can he? If he did that with Lacey?" I wanted so desperately to understand why he'd done it. Why Simon could pretend it had never happened.

Jackson lifted a shoulder in a shrug. "I don't know. I mean, people screw up sometimes. Even if they are in love. We're an imperfect species."

"Screwing up is locking himself in the bathroom when he found out my mom was pregnant. Not hooking up with Lacey."

Jackson's expression turned cloudier than a Tadita rainy day.

"I don't think my mom would forgive him if she found out. I mean, I can't even forgive him and he's not my boyfriend."

Jackson drummed his fingers on the tabletop. "Who knows though? I mean, she really loves him, right? And what if it never happened again?"

I shook my head. I couldn't forgive someone for betraying me like that. Could she?

"Are you and Simon close?" Jackson asked.

"We were. I really liked him. We talked about stuff since he's, you know, black. Like me. And it helped. It sounds dumb. But it helped."

"It doesn't sound dumb."

The waiter walked by our table, taking a tall black man and a black woman to their table. I stared at them. Longingly.

I shook my head sadly. "Well, it doesn't matter. Because now I can barely stand being around him. It makes me crazy. Keeping his secret for him. Protecting him. " I picked up my drink and sipped it to calm myself. "Instead of sharing a heritage, instead of him helping me understand it, he's made me hate him and everything he stands for."

Jackson glanced over at the couple who'd sat far enough away from us so we still had privacy.

"What he did doesn't have anything to do with race."

If I were a dog, the hairs on my back would have stood up. "I know that," I growled. I wasn't stupid. I knew it wasn't an issue about race. "I meant everything he stands for as my mom's boyfriend."

"Maybe you can think of it as not protecting him but protecting your mom?" Jackson said.

I lowered my eyes to the table. "I don't want to be the one to take him away from my new baby brother or sister."

Jackson sat quietly for a moment. "Maybe he just really did screw up, you know? A mistake. He does seem to care about your mom. And the baby. It sounds like he cares about you too."

I stiffened on the booth seat. "So you think it was okay?"

Jackson took his arms off the back of the booth and leaned forward. "No. I'm not defending him or what he did. I'm just saying…"

I shook my head. "It's not right."

"Sometimes things aren't always black and white."

I snorted. "You think I, of all people, don't know that?" I pointed at the skin on my arm. "Black and white. Like me. Like the baby."

Jackson smiled. His mouth opened wider, and he chuckled.

I stared. How could he make fun of this? I instantly regretted my stupid decision to trust him.

"Sorry," Jackson said, but he didn't sound sorry at all, and he didn't even try to wipe the smile off his face.

"It's not funny," I said. I made a fist under the table. I seriously wanted to reach across the table and punch him. God. Thanks to Simon, I'd become a liar and a people smacker.

"Jaz, open your eyes."

I glared at him. "You have a really weird sense of humor, Jackson."

"I guess I should explain. About my grandma."

"That you live with her?" I was about to reach under the table for my guitar and leave Jackson behind. So much for trusting people.

"She's black."

I blinked and stared at him. "What?"

"My grandma is black. I guess my grandpa was a grumpy white guy, but Grams, not so much. My mom was like you. Well, lighter, but the same. She never let me forget it either. Whenever she was drunk, she told me I was 'stained by black blood.' And she was drunk a lot." He rested his elbows on the table and leaned forward. "She died when I was seven."

"Why did you not tell me this?"

"You never asked."

I blinked at him, trying to absorb his story. I had a hard time wrapping my mind around it. How could he have left out this little piece of information about himself?

"I'm sorry. That sounded wrong. I wanted to tell you. But it never seemed to happen. Not the right time or something. But then I told you we would swap secrets someday. And I decided that when you could trust me, I would tell you the truth."

My mouth literally hung open. A mix of emotions filtered through my brain. Denial. Shock. Anger. How could he not tell me? How could he just walk around looking 100 percent white, blending in with everyone else, while I stood out like a zebra in a field of horses? How did I not know this? How did no one know?

I stared at him, studying his skin tone. Light. Slightly tanned. His straight black hair. Not a sign of a curl. Brown eyes. Slender nose. And for a moment, I was overcome with envy. And then I felt a swoop of anger.

"My mom died in a drunk-driving accident. Unfortunately, she was the drunk. Anyhow, after she died, I got tossed into foster care. A few weeks passed, and Grams found out about me and came and got me out. I was her family, she said. She's looked after me since."

My anger vanished. I hadn't bothered to look past the surface of his life. I'd been too wrapped up in myself. I'd assumed his home life was fine, normal, despite his thing with drugs. I'd never once asked him why he lived with his grandma.

"My mom drove drunk all the time, so the good thing was that no one else got hurt. It could have been worse." He smiled but looked sad. "I missed her at first, of course. Even though she'd mostly treated me like crap. She blamed me for my dad leaving. Grams told me he was a redneck. Lily white. He couldn't stand having a 'part-nigger child.' The ultimate hypocrite, really." Jackson tugged on his earring.

My fingers instinctively felt for my charm. I tried to imagine him as a boy. Little. Neglected. At least my grandparents had treated me right. I ached for the little boy he'd been.

"My mom was even too drunk to bother putting me in school on time. I didn't start school until she died. Two years late."

"So that's why you're almost two years older than me. You didn't fail kindergarten?"

Jackson laughed, a hard unpleasant hoot. "You believed that rumor? Kindergarten dropout."

I peeked out at him, hiding behind a curl covering my eye. "Your family sounds worse than mine."

He lifted his shoulder slightly. "It hasn't been so bad. Grams is cool."

"You're close?"

"She doesn't put up with crap from me, but she means well. She's the one who put me into juvie when she found out I was dealing. When I got out, she moved us out of Canada and back here to get me away from my old friends. She lived in Tadita when she was younger and still has friends here."

I looked down at the tablecloth. "You don't look black," I told him. I almost wanted him to be white.

"That doesn't mean squat."

I snorted. "That's debatable. No one knows about you by looking. People take one look at me, and they know I don't belong to either race."

"You belong, Jaz. You're a human being. Color isn't what you are. It's just your shade. You're beautiful. Inside. Where it counts."

I looked down at the table. Yeah. Inside. Where no one could see. Just like Jackson's color.

"That's easy for you to say. How come no one knows then? You can tell me you've never been ashamed of your grandma? You've never worried about people meeting her or judging you for it?"

"Never." Jackson said. "Grams took me in. She was already old but she fought for me. No one knew where my dad was. She told me if they found him, she'd fight for me. What could I possibly be ashamed of? Black is a part of who I am. Just like you."

I chewed my lip. "Not like me."

"I don't try to hide it, Jaz. It just doesn't come up. It's not like I keep my grandma in a closet so no one will find out."

I bit my lip, wishing I had the option of my color pattern not coming up. "What about your grandpa? What was he like? The white guy," I asked, trying to get rid of my uncomfortable and irrational anger with him.

Jackson smiled. "He died before I was born. According to Grams, it was just as well. He'd have killed my dad and blamed him for my mom's death, she said."

I nodded. "My grandpa died when I was thirteen," I told him. "He was my real dad in the ways that mattered. Most people don't get that."

The two of us sat in silence, thinking of our families.

"I'd have told him," I finally said. "About Simon, I mean. My grandpa would have known the right thing to do."

Jackson drummed his fingers on the table and leaned forward. "What do you think that is?" He grabbed my hand.

I stared at his fingers on my own, and my heart played a mean drum solo in my chest. His hand made mine look little, almost dainty.

"What do you mean?" I whispered.

"What do you think the right thing to do is?" Jackson took his hand off mine and reached for his drink, and my fingers missed his immediately.

I thought about his question. "I don't know." But in that moment I realized that in my heart I did. I'd known my answer all along.

"I can't tell. What if my mom rejected the baby if I told her? Like she did with me? My grandma is too old to bring up another baby. I don't want to ruin someone else's life."

"Then don't tell." Jackson's fingers tapped up and down on the checkered cloth, and I listened to the rhythm. It sounded like a song. I smiled in spite of myself. He stopped, and I willed his fingers to move again but they were still on the table.

"I guess you have to trust that it won't happen again." Jackson paused. "What about Lacey?" he asked.

I tucked my hands in my lap. "What about her?"

"Can she keep a secret?"

I leaned back in my seat. "I think so. No one has said a word about it. And she's not exactly the hero in this story."

We sat in silence for a moment, and then the waiter approached our table with a huge piece of apple pie. He placed it in the middle of the table. A scoop of vanilla ice cream had already started melting all over the crust. He put down two forks and left us with a smile.

"Mmm." Jackson said. "Dig in, Jaz. You need to be fattened up."

I gave him a dirty look, but he grinned and dug his fork into the pie, shoving a big piece in his mouth. "Mmm. It's still warm. Come on. Do you know how many girls would kill to be told that they need to be fattened up?"

"Well, not me. I hate being called skinny."

He chewed. "Skinny? Ha! You're perfect, and you know it."

I lifted a fork and shook it at him. "I am not and I do not."

He laughed. "Your forehead gets all wrinkly when you frown like that." He shoved more pie in his mouth.

I took a bite of his pie. The taste of apple and cinnamon warmed my taste buds.

"I can't believe you're part black." I shook my head in disbelief. "I never would have guessed."

He dug his fork back into the pie. "People see what they want to see."

I took another piece of pie and thought about it. We ate in silence for a minute. I knew he'd never gone through what I had. Ignored by the black kids. Ignored by the white ones.

"So your grandma really shipped you to juvie?" I asked.

"Yup. She's tough." He put down his fork and folded his hands, his expression serious. "I've never claimed not to have faults. I've done some stuff. Drugs." He grinned but looked like a boy caught with cookie crumbs on his mouth. "But now I'm back in school. Hell, I'm even holding down a part-time job."

I wanted to ask him if he still dealt drugs. If the phone calls were what I thought. But I couldn't make myself say the words.

He smiled. "Amber knows about juvie. I had to tell her when I applied for the job. Apparently she had some druggie years of her own when she was younger."

"Amber?" I put down my fork, finished with the pie.

Jackson nodded. He dug in. "You want the last bite?"

I shook my head.

"Sure?"

He grinned, scooped it up, and shoved it in his mouth. "So? You want to come to my house and play?"

"Play?"

He nodded at my guitar on the floor. "I do a fierce 'Smoke on the Water.'"

I made a face, sure he was teasing me again. "You do not. I've heard you sing."

He laughed. "Okay. You're right. I play. I didn't say I played well. Not like you. But I play. What do you think I did to keep out of trouble at the Bad Boy School?"

I stared at him, waiting for him to continue.

"Mastered guitar chords, of course. Taught to me by fellow juvenile delinquents."

I scowled. "You're making that up."

He grinned. "Nope. I learned to play guitar in juvie." He leaned back and put his hands behind his head. "I don't want to brag, but I have a custom-made Martin. My own inlay design." He leaned forward, grinning at me. "But I guess you're not interested in seeing it."

"You do not have a Martin." I chewed my lip, almost drooling at the thought of a custom Martin guitar.

"Oh, I do all right. You want to see it?"

chapter thirteen

Jackson drove to the oldest part of Tadita, where the mountains were clearly visible on the horizon. He pulled his car up to an old brick apartment building and parked on the street in front.

"It's not exactly the Ritz, but it's home," he said with a shrug.

The building looked like it had been around for a long time. Old but still in nice condition on the outside.

He turned to me. "You sure you want to bring your guitar in?" he asked. "I don't know if your Alvarez can handle it."

I rolled my eyes. "Another secret. A custom Martin." I wasn't sure I believed him yet.

"I don't want to make it jealous of Marty."

"You named your guitar Marty?" I slung my guitar case over one shoulder, my backpack over the other, and opened the passenger door.

"What was I supposed to call it, Fred?"

I shook my head as we climbed out of the car, and I followed him up a sidewalk lined with cracks. I glanced at the building as Jackson got out his key and opened the glass door, holding it for me to go in first. Inside the lobby, an old orange-and-brown rug covered the floor. The smell in the hallway reminded me of old folks' homes where I'd performed with Grandpa Joe.

We passed a group of elderly couples playing cards around a wooden table in what looked like a games room. Jackson waved at them but kept walking to the elevators even as they stopped their game and craned their heads to get a look at me.

He pressed the Up button, and the door opened right away but took forever to close. He smiled. "It's slow so no one gets stuck. Lots of old people live here." He grinned again. "Grandma will be happy with gossip that I brought a girl home. The whole building will be buzzing."

The elevator sluggishly headed to the fourth floor. When the doors finally reopened, Jackson waited for me to walk out first.

"Apartment 404." He pointed down the hall. "We've got a two-bedroom, which is quite an accomplishment in this building. It's mostly the old married couples on our floor. With cats. Lots of cats."

I smiled but didn't say anything as we walked down the narrow hallway toward the door with the gold numbers nailed on: 404. Jackson dangled his keys, and I had a sudden fit of nervousness. I'd never been to a boy's home alone. Who was I kidding? I'd never been to a boy's home at all.

"Uh. Is your grandma home?" I asked, guessing she wasn't. I hoped she was. Wasn't. Was.

"Nope. Friday is poker night at Dorie's." He laughed. "Don't look so shocked. They're old. Not dead." Jackson unlocked the door and gestured for me to go inside.

I stepped into a small entrance. Directly to the left was a kitchen, and a long mirrored closet door was on the right. I slipped off my shoes on the entrance mat and dropped my backpack on the floor. I avoided my reflection and tiptoed after Jackson down the hallway to the living room. The apartment smelled like an old lady. Musty and floral at the same time. I smiled at the thought of Jackson living here.

"Go and sit," Jackson said, pointing to the couch. "I'll get my guitar. It's behind glass in my room. You want something to drink? Orange juice or water or something?"

"No, thanks." I walked to the overstuffed floral couch and sat, putting my guitar case by my feet. "It's not really behind glass, is it?"

A moment later he joined me in the living room, holding a beautiful acoustic guitar with an amazing design etched into the wood. I jumped up, pressing my hands together and bending forward to inspect the instrument, and forgot my nerves. "Oh, my God. It's gorgeous. You did the design yourself?"

"Yup. And I picked out everything else too. The bridge-pin setting, neck, body wood, all of it. Official Mandolin Brothers original. Marty is sweet." He stroked the body of the guitar, touching the strings lightly and lovingly. And then he held it out.

I licked my lips. "You're sure?" I asked, longing to grab it from his hands. "It must have cost a fortune."

He nodded. "Drug money."

I wasn't sure whether to believe him or not. I couldn't resist the guitar though. My fingers caressed the wood, longing to stroke the strings and bring it to life.

"Go ahead," he told me. "Play."

I went back to the couch and got into position with the guitar. Then with a deep breath, I began to strum. "It's amazing," I whispered, and then my fingers plucked out the melody from a favorite song. After that, I closed my eyes and strummed out the first chord to my song.

Jackson sat beside me on the couch.

I kept playing, realizing his opinion meant more than I wanted it to. Then, still in my zone, I quietly sang the words I'd written.

It was you I saw, and I couldn't close my eyes.
You I saw exposing me to your lies.
What you did makes me bereft
Because instead of facing it I left,
And now I'm alone with no one to trust.
Betray me. Betray you. I must.

When I finished, I opened my eyes. Jackson sat close to me. His dark bangs hung over his face. Without thinking, I reached across the guitar and brushed them back from his forehead.

"You wrote that." A statement. Not a question. He smiled. "You're talented. It's an amazing song. I'm just sorry about what inspired it."

My eyes filled with tears.

"I'm sorry Simon let you down," Jackson said quietly, watching me.

He licked his lips. I stared at them. Moist. Pink. They looked so very, very kissable. Compassion shone in his eyes. For me.

I wanted him to kiss me. And I wanted to kiss him more than I'd wanted anything else in my life. My whole body ached, pleading me to do it. *Be brave for once. Kiss him.* I leaned forward. Jackson's eyes widened, but he didn't move back. I held my breath and kept moving until I touched his soft lips with my own.

The kiss altered my body chemistry. His lips were softer than I'd imagined. Light. I breathed him in, his delicious smell. Tentatively I pressed harder on his lips, and he kissed me back. Almost on its own, my tongue darted out, and I nibbled his bottom lip. My insides quivered, thrilled with the sensation.

And then he pulled away.

Jackson jerked back, ending the moment with a horrible gasp.

My eyes sprung open at the sudden painful parting, as if he'd ripped a Band-Aid off a stinging wound. He jumped up from the couch, glancing around the room like a trapped convict. My body instantly flooded with humiliation even as my lips shook with loss. My head swam. I couldn't speak.

He hadn't wanted to kiss me.

"Man. That wasn't supposed to happen." Jackson said, reaffirming my horror. He practically ran to the kitchen to get away from me. "Play some more. I'll get us a drink. Play."

I touched my lips and lowered my eyes, swimming in shame. In the kitchen Jackson clanked glasses around and babbled. I listened without answering him, feeling empty but horrified. He must think me incapable of friendship with a male. He knew about me and Nathan at Marnie's party, and now, when he'd offered his friendship and the sharing of music and his awesome guitar, I'd pounced all over him. What was wrong with me? Did I really have a need to mess everything up? I remembered what Lacey had said about screwing up friendships.

With a deep sigh, I placed his guitar down beside me on the couch and stood as Jackson walked around the corner holding two glasses filled with ice and water. Probably he wanted to dump it over my head. Calm down my hormones or something.

"Hey. What's up?" he asked, glancing at his guitar.

I swallowed a lump. "I, uh, put your guitar down carefully. Don't worry. I love it. It's awesome, but, um, I have to get going." I stared at the ground. "I kind of forgot I was supposed to help my grandma with some stuff tonight."

"You were?" He walked forward and put the glasses down on the coffee table in front of the couch. "You're sure? Let's have a drink of water first. Talk about this. We need to talk."

I bit my lip and forced a smile. "No. No. It's okay. Really. I'm late. I totally forgot. I have to get going. My grandma is really strict. She'll kill me if I'm any later." I wrung my hands together nervously. "Um. I love your guitar. Thanks for showing me." I coughed. "Uh. I'll get my cell from my backpack and call a cab." I grabbed my guitar case from the floor.

Jackson waved his hand in the air, dismissing me. "Jaz. We really need to talk."

No. I didn't want to do that. Not at all. I didn't need more humiliation. "No. No. I have to go. Now. I'll call a cab."

He crossed his arms. "Forget it. I'll drive you home."

I nodded, embarrassed. Truthfully, I didn't have much cash on me or else I would have insisted.

Jackson reached over and grabbed his guitar from the couch. "I'm sorry…I want to tell you…I have to…"

"No, no," I interrupted. I so did not need an explanation of why kissing me revolted him. I forced a smile. "It's fine. I just have to get home." I took my guitar and hurried to the hallway and slipped on my shoes. I opened the door and stepped out into the main hallway, not wanting to be alone with him for another second. I slung my backpack over my other shoulder, clutching the strap close to my chest.

"Shit. Just a sec," he called and rushed to his room with his Martin. When he came out of the apartment, I dashed toward the elevator as he locked up. I pushed the button and he joined me. I wished I could shrivel up and disappear into a layer of wrinkles, unrecognizable as my seventeen-year-old self and like one of the old people who lived there.

"Hey," Jackson said. "I didn't mean to freak you out. It's not what you think. I have some things to work out."

I cringed, imagining his impending "I only like you as a friend" speech, and attempted a fake laugh. "Don't worry." I jumped as my cell started ringing in my backpack pocket. I'd never been so happy to get a call in my whole life.

I made a big production of answering my call, and the elevator finally arrived. We stepped inside as I said, "Hello?"

"Jasmine. Where are you? You didn't let me know where you were headed after karaoke." Grandma sounded panicky.

I opened my mouth to calm her, but she kept talking.

"It's your mom, sweetie. She's gone into labor. Hard and fast labor."

An image of my mom pulling the baby out like she'd threatened to flashed in my head, and I made a face. "But she's not due for a month," I said stupidly.

"Well, apparently this baby is in a hurry. I'm sure it's because your stubborn mother doesn't want a baby shower. Anyway, it's coming."

"Is she all right? I mean, is the baby okay?" Fear stabbed me. "Where's Mom?"

"They're on their way to the hospital. In Pullayup. Her and Simon. I'm on my way too. I'll pick you up. Are you at Grinds? Lacey said you probably went there after karaoke."

I blushed but spun around and glanced at Jackson. He didn't hide his curiosity. "No. I'm with a friend from work."

"Does she have a car? Can she get you to the hospital?" I didn't bother to correct the mistaken gender of my friend.

"Hold on." I covered the mouthpiece. "Could you drop me off at the hospital instead of home?"

"Of course," Jackson said.

I lifted the phone back to my mouth. "Yup, I can get dropped there. Where do I go? Where do I meet you?"

The elevator doors opened, and Jackson led us toward the part of the street where he'd parked his car.

"The Women's Life Care Center. Go to the triage area and tell one of the nurses your mom was brought in and who you are."

I nodded to the phone. "Is she going to be all right, Grammommy?" My old pet name for Grandma slipped out.

"I think so." Her voice shook slightly. "The baby's early, but they have amazing doctors and facilities so…" She made a sound like a hiccup.

"Don't worry," I said. "She'll be fine."

"I know. I know. God. Your mother never does anything according to plan."

She hung up without saying good-bye.

"The baby?" Jackson opened the passenger door for me and held it, waiting for me to get in.

I put my guitar in the back and climbed in. "It's early." I really wanted the baby to be okay. I sat and lifted a nail to my mouth and started chomping it.

Jackson didn't offer false or empty words. "I'll get you there fast." He looked in the backseat. "You can leave your guitar with me instead of dragging it to the hospital. I'll get it back to you."

I glanced back as he closed the door and went around to the driver side of the car. I wanted to take everything with me and never have to see Jackson again, but dragging the guitar around the hospital wouldn't be appropriate under the circumstances. Jackson opened his door, jumped in, and revved the engine.

"She's going to be okay. Don't worry." He sounded a little scared himself though, as he put his foot on the gas and drove me toward the hospital. We barely spoke the whole way there. I quietly worried about my mom and her baby and looked out the window, trying not to think about the kiss. The horrible, wonderful kiss that might have ruined everything with Jackson. But I didn't even have time to think about that now.

Things were about to change again.

chapter fourteen

I found the triage area in the maternity ward and spotted Grandma slouched over in an oversized chair in the waiting room. She looked older and more tired than usual.

"A boy," she said instead of hello. "You've got a baby brother."

A surge of happiness at the news took me by surprise. "Already?" I asked.

Grandma smiled a little sadly but nodded. "He's tiny, and they're in with him, but he's a fighter."

I swallowed a lump in my throat. I think I loved him already. I hadn't expected that. Grandma wrapped her arms around me. It had been a long time since she'd hugged me like that, but I hung on.

"Your mom's doing pretty good too." Grandma pushed me gently away and wiped underneath my eyes. "No tears. This is happy."

Someone cleared their throat behind us, and I turned and saw that a nurse had approached us.

"You're Jasmine?" she asked in a crisp voice. She didn't sound particularly happy about my name. I bobbed my head in response.

"Your mom is asking for you. Come." Without another word, she turned and started to walk the other way.

Grandma marched beside me. The nurse glanced over. "No. Just her. She wants to see her daughter. Alone."

Grandma stopped. "Oh." Her expression stayed neutral. "Oh. Well, maybe I'll go to the gift store then. See if I can pick up something for the baby. You'll stay with your mom until I get back, Jaz?"

I nodded, nervous. Why'd Mom want to talk to me all alone? The nurse tapped her toe up and down so I followed her white running shoes. From behind, I studied her dyed blond hairstyle, which was glued to her head with hair spray. Her body looked angry, bulging out of the burgundy nurse uniform. The corridor we went down smelled like a doctor's office. Same muffled sounds and baby cries.

We passed the nurses' station and then stepped into a hallway lined with numbered rooms. Women in blue hospital gowns lay in beds in the rooms or sat in rocking chairs beside the beds. Many held tiny babies in their arms. All of them looked tired.

The nurse stopped outside the room at the end of the hall. "She's in there." She gestured at the room with her thumb and scrutinized me. "Your dad is with the baby," she said through pinched lips.

"He's not my dad."

I nervously peeked around the doorway, looking for my mom inside the room.

The nurse tsked and clucked her tongue against the roof of her mouth. "I guess that's not a surprise."

My insides reeled with unease. "What?"

She crossed her arms, and her lips disappeared into a thin line. "Nothing."

She couldn't be implying what I thought.

"Can you please explain what you mean?" She stepped back at the ferocity of my tone. It stunned both of us.

She glared at me. I glared back.

"You know, it's not like I've never seen that look before. But a tiny little baby doesn't deserve that from someone like you."

"Someone like me?"

"You think because he has a black father and a white mother, the baby is bad or evil or something?"

"I don't know what you're talking about." The nurse turned up her nose, but her cheeks got splotchy.

"You know what? I think you do. But it's your problem. Not his." The tiny baby I hadn't even met brought out a protective side of me I hadn't even known existed. I wasn't about to let a stupid nurse label my baby brother.

I stood taller. I decided right then that I'd have to teach him how to handle people like her. Meanwhile, until he was old enough, he'd need someone to stick up for him. I stepped up to the plate. I wouldn't let him deal alone. He'd never be alone. I'd protect him.

Without acknowledging the nurse, I tiptoed inside my mom's maternity room. A blue curtain separated two beds. One was empty, but the bed by the window looked lumpy. I crept toward it.

"Mom?" I whispered.

Her eyes opened, bloodshot and watery as if she'd been on a serious bender.

"Hey," I said, overcome by strange almost motherly feelings for her. I saw the hospital bracelets on her wrist. Two of them. "So you had a baby."

She laughed, but it sounded dry and humorless. "Either that or I got hit by a truck." She sighed as deeply as one of Aretha Franklin's soul-searching songs. "Don't tell Grandma I said that," she told me. "She's probably mad I was only in labor for an hour."

"I hardly think that's what Grandma thinks."

Mom closed her eyes. "Even though he was tiny, it hurt." She paused for a minute. "I hope he's going to be okay. He's really small."

I reached as if to pat her hand, but I pulled back before I touched her. "He'll be okay."

"Simon's in there willing him to good health." She opened her eyes. "He weighs over five pounds. He'll be fine."

Her robotic voice worried me a little. "What's his name?" I asked softly.

She turned her head, looking out the window. "We don't know yet. We haven't agreed on a name. We're talking about it."

I waited, trying to think of something to say. It was like talking to a stranger.

"I wanted to talk to you about something."

I held my breath, waiting to get shit for hitting Simon.

"I'm sorry I haven't been a better mom." Her voice stayed flat, which kind of canceled my relief at not getting in trouble.

"Mom. Forget it. You were young when you had me, and things turned out okay. I mean, I knew you cared and stuff. It was just different."

"I was like a sister. And not always a very good one."

I shrugged. "It doesn't matter. I knew who you were to me."

Tears plopped from my mom's eyes and rolled down her cheeks.

"Of course it matters. I didn't even raise you myself." Her face scrunched up as if she was in pain. "You're such a good kid. You don't even yell at me or complain."

I looked out the window, but the only view was the brick wall of the hospital. "You're emotional from having the baby, that's all. You should rest."

She grabbed my hand, startling me. "If anything happens to me, make sure that Simon is the one to look after the baby."

"Mom, nothing's going to happen to you." I tried to pry my hand away, but she held on.

"But if something does happen. Simon's his dad. Promise. I don't want Grandma raising him."

"Okay, Mom. Okay."

She dropped my hand and closed her eyes again. "Thanks. Thanks, Jaz. I knew I could rely on you." She smiled weakly. "You should see him. He's darker than you. Simon said he's as black as his daddy's behind."

I giggled at the comment as the evil nurse walked into the room. She marched over to the bed without smiling. I wondered if she'd heard us. I moved aside for the nurse to take my mom's pulse and blood pressure.

"Your husband is on his way from the Level Two nursery," she said as she pulled apart the Velcro straps for the blood-pressure monitor.

"He's not my husband."

The nurse glared at her and then at me. "I heard."

I raised my chin. "Well, glad we've got that little detail established. Anything else you want to know?"

The nurse glowered as she grabbed Mom's wrist, placed two fingers on it, and lifted her other hand with the wristwatch on to take Mom's pulse.

"I don't think it's the lack of marriage she disapproves of," I said. "She doesn't like white people who don't stick to their own kind. Or the babies that result."

Mom collapsed farther into her pillows. "Jaz. Don't make trouble."

The nurse's bright red face reminded me of a circus clown. She dropped my mom's hand and wrapped the blood-pressure kit around her arm.

"I'm not making trouble. She's prejudiced."

"I'm not." She glared at me. "Excuse me. I have to take her blood pressure."

I was glad my pressure wasn't being checked. It would be off the charts.

"I'll bring you a robe so you can get up to see the baby," the nurse said to my mom.

She deflated farther into her pillows. "No. I can't. Not yet."

"You need to move around, and your baby needs you." The nurse's voice radiated disapproval. She tapped her nails on the blood-pressure pump.

"She said she can't right now," I interrupted, my voice overly high pitched. Playing grown-up was hard work.

The nurse made a noise in her throat as she made notes in Mom's chart and then gathered her equipment and hurried out of the room.

My mom sat up, wiping under her eyes. "You're doing my dirty work for me now. I'm a terrible mother."

"No, you're not. You need to rest. Don't let that mean nurse bully you."

She sniffled. "I can't even bear to see the baby right now. I don't deserve a baby. He's better off without me in there. Simon can look after him better than I can."

"You're just tired, Mom." I grabbed a Kleenex box from a small table at the end of her bed, and then Simon rushed into the room, sucking all the oxygen from it. My cheeks warmed, remembering the last time I'd seen him. I handed my mom tissues and moved away, leaning back against the windowsill.

"He's doing great, Tara." Simon bent down and kissed her cheek. "He's going to be okay."

"I know," Mom answered, her eerie voice stripped of emotion.

"Hey, Slugger." Simon winked. "So you're a big sister."

"Congratulations," I said formally.

His grin was as wide as his face. "I'm a dad!" He rushed forward and grabbed me, lifting me up and spinning me in a circle. Apparently he'd forgiven me. I wished I could say the same. I went rigid, waiting to be put down, but Simon didn't seem to notice. Finally he plopped me down.

"He's small and he's early, but he's going to be okay." He grinned as if he'd done something really amazing.

I tried not to smile but gave in.

"You want to meet him?" he asked me. He glanced at Mom. "Is that okay, Tara? Can I take Jaz down to see him? You can stay here and rest."

I shook my head, but Mom nodded, almost disappearing into her pillows and closing her eyes again.

"Come on." Simon leaned over and kissed Mom's cheek and then grabbed my hand and pulled. "Come on. I'll introduce you to your brother. Get some sleep, Tara. I'll take Jaz to meet our baby."

Before I could protest, he tugged me out of the room. "I'm sorry about the other day, Jaz. I understand why you blew up at me. Your dad—and then me, all complaining about your mom, and well, I'm sorry. I should never have said anything to you. It was stupid." He dragged me along. "Let's forget it, okay?"

He babbled on, giving me too many details about my mom's water breaking at work and her fast delivery, her pushing starting in the car. When we reached the neonatal room, his voice lowered.

"He's in the NICU. Some of the babies inside are really small, but he won't be here for long. The nurses and doctor are concerned about his liver. But he'll be okay. Come on. He's over here."

He tugged me past some heartbreakingly fragile babies attached to tangled wires, tubes, and IVs. The room was a blur of machines, lights, and alarms.

"That's him." He pointed inside an incubator.

I gasped. I gazed down at my tiny brother. Patches of kinky black hair covered his teeny head, which seemed too big for his thin body. Little probes poked into his dark skin. His eyes were squeezed shut, and his head lay sideways as if breathing was a challenge for someone so little. My heart melted like chocolate in sunshine. Sweet. Delicious.

As I stared down at him, a surge of love and protectiveness pulsed through my blood.

My baby brother. I loved him.

"He's gorgeous," I whispered to Simon. "He's so tiny."

"I know," he answered.

The two of us stood in front of the incubator, staring in amazement at the little creature. Before long, Grandma arrived to see her grandson. We all stood in awe, admiring him in his little incubator.

"It's late," Grandma finally said. "They'll be kicking us out."

We went back to Mom's room to say good-bye, but she didn't open her eyes while we were there. We left the hospital, and Simon headed home to sleep for a few hours and to pick up baby supplies and a change of clothes for Mom.

I was worried about my mom, but Grandma told me she'd be fine. I had no choice but to believe her.

chapter fifteen

"Good morning," Grandma said when I finally crawled out of bed. It was past noon.

Grandma sat perched on her stool at the kitchen island with the Tadita *Standard* unfolded in front of her. "I made some muffins. Help yourself." She pointed to a plate stacked with homemade baking on the kitchen table. I sniffed the air. Apple cinnamon.

"Simon called earlier. The baby's doing better than they expected. He shouldn't be in the hospital too long. Maybe two weeks."

I waited to see if she'd say more, but obviously Simon hadn't mentioned our fight at McDonald's. And most likely wouldn't.

"That's good, isn't it?" I asked.

"It's good," Grandma answered.

We smiled at each other as I headed for the fridge and pulled the door open to root inside for milk.

"Too bad the same can't be said for your mom." Grandma sighed.

I grabbed the carton of milk and glanced back at Grandma. "What'd you mean?"

"The baby needs her, but she's acting all dramatic and helpless."

I didn't comment. I'd learned to stay out of the struggles between Mom and Grandma. Grandma could be pretty hard on Mom sometimes. Grandma was happy about the baby, but that didn't stop her from being critical. In my opinion, my mom deserved a bit of a break. She'd just given birth.

I poured myself a glass of milk.

"You going to work today?" Grandma asked.

"Yup. At three," I told her.

"Oh. They're sending your mom home today. Simon said she hasn't slept a wink in the hospital." She made a tsking sound.

I ignored her, focusing on my milk, and went to the kitchen table and sat, reaching for a muffin.

"Your mom hasn't even visited the baby in the NICU."

I lowered my head and bit off a chunk of muffin.

"He should be bonding with his mother. Poor baby." Grandma shook her head and tsked again. She flipped a page of her paper. "At least she's pumping milk for him. She said she's going to breast-feed."

I chewed and shrugged. I had no desire to get involved in a debate about Mom's parenting skills. Grandma waited for encouragement to go on, but I said nothing.

"Would you like to go and visit before your shift at work?"

I didn't want to face the evil nurse or deal with Simon. "No. I have calculus homework I need to finish and I have to work tomorrow too."

Grandma nodded. "I need Grandpa's car to go to the hospital," she reminded me.

"Maybe you could drop me off. I could study at Grinds before my shift."

I'd done more than my fair share of homework at Grinds.

Grandma glanced at the clock. "Can you be ready to go in an hour?"

"Yup. I'll shower and change after I eat."

She pulled out a new section of the paper and laid it flat in front of herself.

"Oh. I almost forgot. Some handsome boy dropped off your guitar this morning. Said he was a friend of yours from work."

My face heated up. "Oh."

"Why'd he have your guitar?"

I dropped my eyes. "I left it with him last night. He drove me to the hospital."

"You were with a boy after karaoke last night?"

I didn't answer since it seemed rather obvious. Her eyes didn't leave me.

"Oh. Well, he seemed polite. He said to tell you hello."

She had no idea how polite. So polite he'd managed not to laugh in my face when I'd practically thrown myself at him. I felt like puking and put the muffin down.

I was glad when Grandma turned her attention back to her paper.

I left the kitchen and found my cell and called Ashley. She didn't pick up, and I didn't leave a message. I'd handle it on my own. Like I always did.

• • •

Not in the mood for caffeine, I ordered a juice from Amber and settled into a quiet corner table to get to work on my homework. My heart skipped a beat thinking about seeing Jackson in a few hours when he'd be working with me. Talk about getting signals wrong. I'd have to act like nothing had happened.

Halfway through a calculus equation, I was startled by a voice in the coffee line.

I glanced up. Jackson was in line, leaning against the counter and casually chatting with Amber at the cash register. My heart flopped, and I chomped harder on my pencil. He laughed and flicked back his hair with an unconscious toss of his head. In line behind Jackson, an annoyingly gorgeous girl with long blond hair was eyeing his butt. I couldn't blame her. It was a butt worth staring at.

Jackson flashed a sexy half grin at Gorgeous Girl, and the orange juice in my stomach curdled. I watched as he placed a hand on her back and leaned down to whisper something in her ear. She smiled adoringly up at him, and then he turned to Amber and ordered coffee. Two coffees.

Amber glanced over and caught my eye and quickly looked away. I stared down at my math book, mortified. I wished I could fade into the background. Why had coming early to do homework seemed like a good idea?

I pretended to be absorbed in my work, praying somehow that Jackson wouldn't notice me tucked into the corner. I barely moved or breathed, hoping he'd take his coffee and the girl to go.

"Jaz?"

Wincing, I sucked in a breath, forced a smile, and looked up. Jackson and the girl approached my table. Jackson's cheeks looked unusually red and his face uncomfortable as if his underwear was scratchy. I hoped his underwear crawled with ants. Red ants that bit.

They got closer. The pretty blond gaped at me with wide, curious eyes. Her eyelashes were long and coated in mascara.

"Who's your friend?" she asked. She didn't seem jealous to meet me though. As if it would be absurd that someone like me would be a threat. Someone like me would never practically stick my tongue down Jackson's throat.

Jackson didn't seem to hear her. His mouth stiffened.

"Hey. I thought you didn't work until later," he said to me.

"I don't." I glanced down at my work. "Homework." I sneaked another look at the gorgeous creature at his side.

"Oh." He brushed his bangs back. "How's your mom? She had her baby okay?"

I nodded. "Yeah. She's okay."

"Your mom had a baby?" the girl asked me. "That is totally weird."

"My mom is only thirty-three," I told her.

"Wow. My mom's like fifty. I can't imagine her having a baby." She scrunched up her pretty face.

I nodded and glanced down, pretending to mull over my math homework.

"You got your guitar okay?" Jackson asked.

"Guitar?" the annoying chick chirped.

I looked up.

"Uh. This is Carrie," he said to me. Based on the look on his face, his underwear had gotten even scratchier. "This is Jaz," he said to Carrie.

"I'm his girlfriend from Whistler," the blond told me, holding out her free hand to inspect her nails as if explaining she'd just come in first in a beauty pageant.

I swallowed. His girlfriend?

"Oh. Well, I only know Jackson from work," I babbled. "Barely."

Not well enough to know he had a girlfriend. "Um. Nice to meet you, Carrie." I pushed myself up, needing to escape, no matter how rude that was. "I have to go to the bathroom. Excuse me."

I hurried past them, almost bumping Carrie's coffee right out of her perfect hand as I squeezed past. Her perfect Caucasian hand.

"Jaz, hey, wait," Jackson called as I took off for the washroom.

"Jackson, what are you doing?" Carrie demanded in a huffy voice. "What's wrong with you?"

I picked up my pace until I reached the safety of the women's washroom. I burst through the door and dove into a stall, locking it behind myself and panting with humiliation.

I dropped my butt on the toilet seat and put my head in my hands. A few minutes later, feet stepped inside the bathroom and stopped outside the stall.

"Jaz?"

Amber.

I groaned.

"He's gone," she said softly. "They left."

I nodded. "Okay," I said out loud. "Thanks."

"You should talk to him. Don't jump to conclusions," Amber said.

I snorted under my breath. "It's no big deal. We're just friends," I called.

Amber didn't answer but she left. A few minutes later, I skulked out of the stall. I returned to my table, packed up my homework, and hurried out the front door and walked home. I phoned on the way home and told Amber I wouldn't be able to work that night. She didn't even give me trouble.

At home I took the phone off the hook, shut off my cell, and went straight to bed.

• • •

Sunday afternoon, I reported for work grouchy and tired. Of course, Lacey and I were working together, and she decided to make it worse.

"Hey, Jaz. Did you hear Jackson brought his girlfriend to work yesterday?" She watched as I punched in for work, one hand on her hip and the other flicking back her blond hair. "I totally didn't know he had a girlfriend in Whistler, did you?"

I placed my time card in its slot.

"My mom had her baby," I said, staring at Lacey and willing her to shut up.

"Oh. Yeah. I heard that." Lacey fussed with the strings on the back of her apron. She smiled. "That's great. How's the baby doing?"

"He was early, so he's pretty little. They're watching his liver development. But Simon said he'll be okay."

"How about your mom?"

"Tired." I narrowed my eyes. "Simon's totally psyched about being a dad. Grandma said he's handing out chocolate cigars to everyone."

Lacey glanced toward the restaurant area. "That's great. I mean, I guess you're a big sister now, huh?"

I pictured the tiny little baby, and an intense surge of love stole the breath right out of me. "He looks like Simon."

"Mmm? Well, great."

Lacey twirled her hair as I pulled my apron off the hook and tied it around my back.

"So?" she asked. "Did you know Jackson had a girlfriend?"

She'd gotten back to what she really wanted to talk about. She knew me well enough to know I was crushing hard on Jackson. What she didn't know was that I had unwillingly joined her club. The making-out-with-taken-guys club. And it felt horrible.

I ignored her and stomped toward the coffee pit. She followed, yapping close on my heels. "I didn't know he had a girlfriend. I heard she's really pretty. A cheerleader type."

I spun around. "Shut up, Lacey. For once, just shut the hell up."

We stared at each other, shocked by the vehemence in my voice. I breathed as if all the air had been squeezed from my lungs. "I don't give a shit about Jackson or his stupid girlfriend," I lied. "You're concerned about the wrong thing. Again. Jackson didn't tell me he had a girlfriend, okay? Does that make you happy? Because Jackson's an asshole? Well. So are you. You're both assholes and you're both shitty friends." I stared at Lacey, hating her as if she somehow had something to do with this too.

"I'm an asshole?"

We both spun around.

Jackson cleared his throat and narrowed his eyes, peering at me from the other side of the counter. "And a shitty friend?"

"You are," I shouted and clenched my fists. Now that I'd taken off the lid, everything wanted to boil out. "I'm sick of you people acting like a bunch of children."

I pointed at Lacey. "You with my mom's boyfriend." I pointed at Jackson. "And you not bothering to tell me you had a girlfriend." I reached back, untied my apron, pulled it off, and threw it on the floor. "And who the hell cares? I'm leaving."

It felt as if I was watching myself perform in some weird play. Jaz Evans didn't act like this. "Tell Amber I'm sorry I took off on my shift," I called.

I rushed out of the coffee shop and broke into a run.

chapter sixteen

I was running, heading toward a side street, when a car pulled up and idled behind me.

"Jaz. Hey, Jaz," Jackson called.

I didn't answer him but ran faster.

"Your legs are pretty long, but I don't think you can outrun my car."

"I don't see why not. It's a piece of shit," I yelled.

"Ouch. I'm an asshole, and now my car is a piece of shit?"

My legs ached from running too fast and my lungs burned.

"Can you stop? I really need to talk to you."

I kept going.

"Jaz, come on," Jackson pleaded.

I puffed harder.

"I'm sorry," he called and cleared his throat. "That I didn't warn you about Carrie."

"I don't want to talk to you about your stupid girlfriend. I want to get some exercise." I yelled. My breath came in short puffs. "Go away."

"You're running in your work uniform, in case you forgot."

"So?"

"Well. You may have excellent running form, but you look kind of dorky," he called.

I stopped dead in my tracks, forcing Jackson to slam on his brakes to keep from hitting me.

"Don't you dare tell me I look dorky," I yelled, panting and grabbing my side. Stupid stitch.

He shifted his car into park.

"Well, you kind of do," he pointed out.

His stereo played faintly inside the car. I heard a muffled Green Day song. Figured. White-guy music.

"Well, at least I look like one. I am a dork. Look at you in your white-guy car, listening to white-guy music. Dating a blond with boobs. You're a total faker." My hand dug into my side, trying to stifle the cramp. My eyes got teary, and that made me even madder.

Jackson opened his car door and stepped outside. "A faker?"

"No," I yelled at his face. "I don't want to hear crap about accepting myself for who I am. You have the option of blending in. I don't."

"No one's asking you to," he said.

"Don't patronize me," I snarled. He took a step toward me, but I backed away.

"What do you want from me, Jackson? A close-up view of what it's like to look black and live in the white world? Well, too bad. I'm not going to give it to you. You're on your own."

He leaned against his car door, his arms crossed. "I want to be your friend. I like you. You're not making it easy to get to know you, but..."

"But what?" I interrupted before he embarrassed me further. "I screwed it up and thought it was more and threw myself at you? So you had to haul out your girlfriend to show me how stupid I was? Well, guess what? You're right. I am stupid. But everyone makes mistakes, and that was the biggest mistake I ever made. Kissing you."

I shook my head, my humiliation and his pity making me furious. Pain and anger I'd been holding in forever rose to the surface. I was humiliated and tired of it. Tired of people pushing me down. Letting me slide under while they just watched. I was tired of holding it all in. Pretending nothing bothered me.

And at that moment, I wanted to make him hurt as much as I did. So I went for blood. "You know what's sad, Jackson? I once promised my grandpa I'd stay away from people like you. Druggies." I spit the word out like it was dirt muddying my tongue. Like he was beneath me in any real or imagined social ranking.

"I've heard you on your phone. Setting up pickup times, arranging things, trying to hide it from me. I know you're still dealing drugs."

He opened his mouth, but I raised my hand to silence him.

"My grandpa would have *hated* you. He wouldn't have wanted us to be friends. And you know what? He would have been right. I'm sorry I'm a dork and that I kissed you. Let's just forget it ever happened. The funny thing is not only should I never have done that, but I shouldn't even be friends with someone like you. You're probably the only person I've ever met who isn't even good enough for me." Jackson took a step back.

In the back of my mind, the ugliness of my words horrified me, but suppressed anger spewed out of me, propelling the poison onward. "Go back to your white-ass girlfriend and deal your drugs and leave me alone. I don't need you hanging around me to try to see what it's like to actually look black. You don't deserve to claim that part of your heritage. At least I'm not trying to pass myself off as something I'm not. You're not white, but you're not black either. You're not anything."

Jackson's expression didn't change. He didn't say a word. He pushed off the door of his car. He hopped inside without looking at me. He threw the car into drive and peeled off, leaving the smell of burning rubber in the air.

I watched him go and burst into tears, feeling as hateful as everyone who'd ever judged me for the color of my skin.

• • •

I went home and typed up a resignation letter, then marched back to the coffee shop and into Amber's office. Some of my bravado faltered when Amber smiled at me, but I held out the piece of paper. "Sorry for ditching my shift."

"What's this?" Amber asked as she scanned the page.

I waited while she read my resignation notice.

"I won't pretend I'm not disappointed," Amber said when she'd finished reading. "But I won't pretend I'm surprised either." She leaned back in the chair, her head at an angle, watching me. "You want to talk about it?"

I bit my lip and shook my head.

"You sure, honey? I heard you're having trouble with Lacey, and I'm not sure what's going on with you and Jackson."

"I'm sorry. I just have to quit," I told Amber and struggled not to cry.

Amber muttered under her breath. “Tell you what,” she said finally. “You’re a great employee.” She narrowed her eyes. “Well, outside of your last couple of shifts. I’ll keep this resignation letter on file, and I’ll take you off the schedule. But if you ever want to come back to work, I’ll consider this a leave of absence.”

I nodded, working hard to keep back tears. “Thanks, Amber. I’m really sorry about my leaving you like this.” I swiveled and raced from the office.

• • •

I avoided Jackson. The avoiding part was simple. I didn’t work at Grinds anymore, and I talked to my principal and teachers, explaining about my mom having a preemie baby and needing me. I got all my English homework emailed to me. Years of being a good student paid off, because they excused me from classes without batting an eye.

I stayed away from Ashley too. Whatever questions she might have, I didn’t have answers.

Instead, excuses rolled off my lips when she called. My mom needed my help, I told her. I didn’t even flinch as I spit out the lies. I skipped classes, and no one said a word about it. Everyone at school believed I was a responsible young lady, helping out my mom.

I went to see Mom a couple of times after she brought the baby home, but she was jittery and nervous, and being around her made me feel worse. She worried that she wasn’t sleeping. She complained about being stressed about breast-feeding. I felt sorry for her but I didn’t know how to help. I didn’t know what to say.

She wasn’t herself, and neither was I, and I didn’t know how to reach her. Grandma told me Mom’s behavior was normal and that she'd get over it. Baby blues, she called it. I couldn't imagine how Mom had coped with being my age and going through that with me. Of course, back then she'd handed me over to Grandpa and Grandma. And as much as I liked the little baby Mom still hadn't named, he was stirring up feelings in me. I was having a hard enough time dealing with my own life, so I avoided theirs too.

What flattened me the most was Jackson. Finding out he had a girlfriend had crushed me. I'd had it bad for him, way worse than I'd even thought. The girlfriend thing crushed me. Hollowed out my heart.

But there was no excuse for the things I'd said to him. I didn't even know who I was anymore. To punish myself, I wouldn't allow myself music. I stared at the walls and dwelled on Jackson and Carrie. I imagined Jackson kissing her, not running away. Playing her songs on Marty. Badly, but still. I deserved to hurt after the ugly things that had spewed from my lips. I'd been aiming to wound him, but I'd hit at an amazingly low level.

It embarrassed me, but at the same time I missed him so much that I felt numb. I missed his stupid singing at work. I missed his dumb jokes.

I wasn't hungry, and nothing interested me. I pretended to be sick, but after a few days of me missing school, Grandma stopped buying my story about a flu bug and insisted I go back.

When I got to school, I headed down the hallway toward the library to study for a missed English test. Someone tapped my shoulder, and I turned.

Ashley glared at me. I pulled earbuds from my ears. Even though

I didn't have music playing, the earbuds gave me an excuse to ignore everyone around me. Like a celebrity using a cell phone to hide from paparazzi.

"Hey, you scared me." I smiled at her hair. The ends were black. I realized how much I'd missed her in my self-induced exile. "Nice tips."

She didn't smile back. "Where have you been? I haven't talked to you or seen you in days. I've been texting you, and you haven't answered."

Students rushed past us, bumping into us as they headed for classes and lockers. Ashley pushed my shoulder and moved us off to the side of the herd.

I glanced longingly at the center of the chaos, wishing I could dart back inside the moving stream of bodies and away from a heart-to-heart chat.

"My mom brought her baby home," I told Ashley instead of admitting I'd ignored her messages. "He got out of the hospital early."

"I know that. I heard, and that's great." She scowled. "But where have you been?"

I shrugged. "I've been helping her out." Another lie. "She's kind of a mess." She was a mess, but I wasn't doing much to help her. I watched a group of freshman girls pass by us without even looking at us. We were too uninteresting, I guess. They had no clue.

"You've missed an entire week of English."

I stared longingly at the dwindling backs of the kids in the hall. There was no one else around us. "I know. I'll catch up on what I missed. I was actually just heading to the library to study. I should go."

Ashley scowled. "This is so not like you."

I lifted a shoulder. "Well, there are extraordinary circumstances. The principal cleared me from the classes I missed, and I met with my teachers to work it all out. They're letting me make up what I missed. My mom needs me."

Ashley licked her lips. "Well, I'm still really pissed off at you."

I frowned. "I told you I've been busy. I'm sorry I didn't return your texts."

"You're full of shit."

Great. There went my last friend. I looked away from her and glanced longingly down the hall toward the library, wishing I'd made a dash for freedom when the hall had been full of kids to hide behind.

"Jackson told me what you said. That he didn't deserve his black heritage. And that you called him a fake white person. What do you want him to do? Wear a sign to tell the world that his grandma is black?" Ashley didn't have to vocalize her unhappiness with my stupid words. It was etched in her features and in the air between us.

My cheeks warmed, thinking of the low blows I'd delivered.

"Why were you even talking to Jackson about it?" I demanded instead of admitting what an idiot I'd been.

"We've been having lunch together. He told me about what happened."

I stared at her. "You have lunch with Jackson?"

"Well, you haven't been around. And he's a nice guy. He's funny."

"Great. I'll be spending the rest of my senior year alone," I mumbled.

"Jaz. Will you stop thinking only about yourself for once?"

Her words slapped against my face, as hurtful as if she'd hit me with her bare hand. I dropped my gaze to the floor. Humiliated. I wanted to tell her about what I'd been carrying around. How I'd been thinking about nothing but Simon and my mom for the last few months.

"You did this to yourself, Jaz. No one did it to you. And I'm really surprised." I bit my lip trying not to cry. "I gotta say I'm more than a little disappointed in you."

"Well you're not the only one, okay? I was mad. I got carried away." I brushed back a curl from my face and stared at a crack in the floor.

"So how exactly does someone fake being white?" Ashley asked in a proper tone.

"It was stupid. I didn't mean it."

"Do you think it really matters that he looks white?" I bit my lip, trying not to cry.

"Well, do you?" she asked.

I frowned and looked up at her, not used to this side of Ashley. "It does to some people."

"But are those the people you care about, Jaz? The question is, does it matter to you?"

I sighed and looked up at her. At the unfamiliar glint in her eyes. Disappointment. Disappointment with me.

"It feels like he has it easier or something."

"You mean easier than you?"

"Fine. Okay. You're right. I'm jealous. He fits in. He looks like everyone else." I looked around the hallway, wishing a teacher would come and chase us away, but where were they when you needed them?

"You think I'm not okay because I'm not like everyone else."

"*No*. No. That's not what I meant." I ran my fingers through my hair and scratched at my head.

"So tell me what you meant."

"I don't know. I feel bad. Okay? I shouldn't have said that to him. He has a black heritage as much as I do. I know that." I jutted my chin out. "But the drug part is true," I said, wanting to be right about something. "I've heard him making deals on his phone. Anyhow, he has a girlfriend, so why does he even care what I think?" I stepped away from Ashley, ready to move on, to hide in the library and block out this conversation. I wanted to be alone. I'd been without friends before. I could certainly do it again.

Ashley jumped in front of me, blocking my way. When I tried to wiggle by, she grabbed me. "You know what? It's not the color thing. Or even the drug thing. It's the girlfriend thing that's made you crazy. You're totally jealous."

The bell rang as I opened my mouth to tell her she was wrong. In other words, to lie some more.

She cursed under her breath. "I can't miss geography. I have an exam. I have to go." She let me go but frowned and shook her finger in my face. "We need to talk. Can you meet me later?"

I shrugged.

"Text me. I'll miss my swim practice if I have to." She turned and started to run. "Hey," she called over her shoulder as she hurried off in the opposite direction. "What did your mom name your brother?"

"She didn't yet," I called back. "He's still generic."

"Still?"

She frowned but disappeared around a corner as she dashed toward her classroom. I lifted my earbuds to tune out the world again, but before I slipped them in my ears, my cell vibrated. I checked call display. It was my mom. Again.

I picked up the phone.

"Jaz. Help me," she cried into the phone. "Come quick. I think I'm dying."

chapter seventeen

I ran up the front steps of Mom's house and unlocked the door. "Mom!" I shouted, flicking off my running shoes on the front doormat.

Muffled baby cries wailed from upstairs like an alarm. My heart thumped, and I almost wished I'd never picked up her phone call so I didn't have to deal with this. Sure, I was worried about her, but I knew she wasn't dying. I also knew she wasn't okay.

"Mom."

There was no answer. The baby shrieks didn't stop, so I dashed up the stairs, following the noise to the baby's room.

I stopped in the doorway. Mom sat hunched over in her rocking chair beside the crib, her hands covering her ears. Her hair was greasy and dirty. It hung down in her eyes as she rocked herself back and forth as if she was in a trance. The baby lay in his crib, screeching and clearly unhappy at being ignored.

"Mom?"

She didn't even look up. My heartbeat echoed louder in my ears.

"Shouldn't you do something about the baby's crying?"

She rocked harder. She didn't make eye contact with me but just shook her head back and forth, faster and harder.

I tiptoed to the crib and peered inside. The baby's face was scrunched up and angry, his tiny mouth wide open, his eyes shut tight like my mom's. The wails coming out of his little body were loud, annoying, and broke my heart.

I looked into his pissed-off little face. "Shh, baby, shhh," I whispered, looking back at my mom for encouragement.

She kept rocking.

With sweaty palms, I reached in and poked the baby's still too skinny belly. I touched his soft yellow sleeper and he cried. I tentatively reached down and placed a hand under his little body. I remembered about making sure to support his head with the other hand and then lifted him. The crying continued.

His tiny body weighed almost nothing, but he thrust his body back and stiffened, pushing against my hands with surprising strength. Instinctively I cuddled him closer to calm him, and I started to rock back and forth.

"There, there," I whispered. "It's okay, baby."

His face relaxed for a moment as if he were searching his memory banks for my voice. As the wailing subsided, I blew out a breath and glanced over at my mom. She didn't look at me but kept rocking. Back and forth, back and forth.

The baby seemed to understand something was wrong. His mouth opened again, and the siren started up.

"You hungry?" I asked him.

He shuddered and hiccuped. I shushed and cooed, and for a moment, his screeching stopped. I pulled him closer, and his tiny body warmed my arm like a little furnace. My heart melted a little more despite his racket.

"Mom?"

I glanced at her. Her eyes remained unfocused, gazing at the floor. She'd wrapped her arms around herself.

Her mouth moved a little. She shook her head back and forth mouthing, "No. No."

I crept closer, cradling the baby. With one hand I grabbed my mom's shoulder and shook. She shrank back as if my hand had scalded her. Her head snapped back and forth, faster and more violently. A wail emanated from deep in her soul. It started softly but intensified, reminding me of a wounded animal.

I froze, listening to her moan. As if he sensed everyone's distress, the baby began to shriek again, not a timid, shy sound. My mom's voice got louder, competing.

My forehead and underarms were slick with sweat. "Shh…there, there," I said out loud, my eyes alternating between the baby and Mom. Neither calmed down.

"Mom? What's wrong?" I called over the noise.

Her guttural shrieks stopped, but she rocked harder in her chair and wrapped her arms around herself as if trying to squeeze her insides out.

"I can't. I can't. I can't," she chanted softly.

I swayed and shushed the baby while my mom repeated the words over and over. The baby hiccuped and then quieted again, his little eyes beginning to flutter with sleep. I stopped swaying and crept toward my mom, but his eyes flew open, and the cries resumed.

I really wanted to hand the baby over and run from the room.

"Mom." I swayed the baby again, trying to calm him. "You can't what?"

She was supposed to stop the crying, not me, but she continued to hug herself, repeating her words over and over and over.

"I can't. I can't. I can't."

The baby's eyes closed and his body stilled to a quiet breathing rhythm, but I didn't dare stop swaying.

"Do this," she said. "I can't do this."

"What?" I didn't know what she meant. She was freaking me out. "What can't you do?"

She lifted her arms and swept them upward, gesturing around the entire room. "This. I can't do this." She ground her teeth together and began rocking again, shaking her head and muttering, "No. No. No. No. I can't. Can't." Her voice sounded dead, as if she'd cut out her emotions.

"I'm going to call Grandma. Okay, Mom?"

She didn't stop rocking. "Take the baby away." She wailed again, uttering a wounded cry that was barely human.

Panic pooled in my stomach. A bead of sweat dripped from my forehead onto the baby's yellow sleeper, but it was quickly absorbed by the fleece.

She wasn't okay, not at all. "I'll be right back, Mom. Will you be okay?"

She didn't answer or look at the baby. Her motions didn't stop.

I carried my brother from the bedroom and closed the door behind me. As I hurried down the stairs, he started whimpering again. It intensified my feelings of inadequacy. I didn't know how to look after a tiny baby.

"Are you hungry?" I asked, hoping by some miracle that he'd

grasp speech really, really early and tell me what he needed. "Do you need a clean diaper?"

At the bottom of the stairs, I lifted him in the air the way I'd seen Mom do. "You are so going to hear about this when you're a teenager." I sniffed at his tiny butt. Nothing foul.

I spotted a pacifier in the baby's playpen in the middle of the living room. I hadn't noticed what a mess the place was when I'd rushed in, but now the chaos struck me as odd. Usually my mom was the neatest person around. Baby or no baby.

I balanced my brother in one arm and reached inside the playpen for his pacifier. When I held it up, he stopped fussing and wrapped his lips around it. His little body quivered and shook, but he began to calm down.

"There. That's better, isn't it, buddy?" I looked around. "Okay, I'm going to phone Grandma and see what we should do." I went to the couch and sat, settling him in my arm and managing to dial the phone at the same time.

Grandma picked up. "Tara?" she said, sounding angry. "What now?"

"No, it's me," I shifted the now contented baby in my arms.

"Jasmine? What are you doing there? Aren't you supposed to be in school? I don't want you missing more classes because of your mom."

"Mom called me at school. She was freaking out." I peered into the baby's innocent face, wondering if he'd remember any of this. I hoped not. "Something's wrong with her. She's acting really weird. It's bad. I think you should come over."

Grandma made a clucking noise. "She's fine. She just needs to take some responsibility. She wants everyone else to do the work for her.

It's not easy, but this time she can look after the baby herself. She's thirty-three years old. I'm too old to raise another baby."

"But she's really freaked out, Grandma. I don't think it's normal."

"She's a drama queen. She hasn't even named him yet, for goodness sake. Leave her with the baby. Go back to school. She'll handle it if we make her."

She was wrong about this. I felt it. "But I don't think she can. I don't think I should leave her alone."

"No buts. It's her son. She's a big girl. You're contributing to the problem by running over there whenever she calls. I want you to go back to school," Grandma ordered.

"She called me and said she was dying."

"I mean it. Go back to school. I'll see you at home in a few hours." She hung up the phone without saying good-bye.

I shook my head, angry with both of them now. "Welcome to our world, little brother," I whispered to the sleeping baby.

I carried him back up the stairs and peeked inside the baby's bedroom door.

"Mom?"

Her face looked pale and drained. She hadn't stopped rocking.

"Why don't you try and have a nap? I'll look after the baby for awhile, okay?"

Mom's eyes filled with tears. "I can't sleep. I can't. I've tried. But I can't." Her voice buzzed with desperation.

"Well, you need to rest at least. Go lie down. I'll take care of him."

Mom nodded, looking relieved, like a little girl afraid of getting in trouble. "There's formula downstairs," she whispered. "Could you feed him?"

"I thought you were breast-feeding?" I asked.

"I can't." Mom wailed, her eyes wide with panic. "I've tried and tried. I'm a terrible mother. I can't do it." Her voice went up, and she started to cry again. "Everybody says I should be able to do it, but I can't."

"Mom, Mom, it's okay. I just thought you were. It's no big deal. It's all good."

She sniffled and tried to calm herself.

"It's okay. What do I need to do?"

"There's sterilized bottles and nipples in the sink. And pre-made formula in the pantry. Give him seven ounces. Don't forget to burp him." Her voice sounded methodical but almost normal.

"Okay, Mom. Go lie down. I can handle it."

I waited as she shuffled out of the nursery looking older than Grandma and moving slowly down the hallway. She disappeared into her bedroom.

"Thanks," she whispered before closing the door behind her.

I stared at the door until the baby spit out his pacifier, and a low-grade wail started.

I studied the little unhappy face. "You're hungry?"

We went downstairs to the kitchen, and I fixed up a bottle. I took him to the couch and started to feed my baby brother for the first time. Gradually, with his lips still on the bottle, he fell asleep in my arms. I stared at his sleeping face. I tasted my love for him. And bitter fear.

I got up and placed him down in his playpen crib, like I'd seen Grandma do, and tiptoed up the stairs. I opened the door to Mom's room, hoping she was sleeping.

She lay on her back, her eyes wide open, staring at the ceiling.

"Mom?"

"I should never have had this baby," she said without looking at me. "Who did I think I was? He'd be better off without me." She crumpled her body up in a fetal position, squeezing her eyes shut.

I stepped inside her room, my heartbeat speeding up. "Mom, that's crazy. Come on."

She didn't answer.

I walked to the side of the bed, leaned down, and touched her forehead. It was clammy and sweaty.

"Mom? You okay?"

"No," she whispered. "I can't do this."

I patted her shoulder but knew how she felt. I didn't think I could handle it either. "I'm going to call Simon."

She didn't protest so I left the bedroom and hurried downstairs to the kitchen phone. I dialed Simon's cell number, but voice mail picked up.

"Simon, when you get this message, call home. Mom's acting really, um, weird. I'm here, but I'm worried. Really worried." I hung up and went to check on the baby.

I picked him up, toting him with me to the couch. I sat holding him in my arms and wishing I could protect him from whatever was happening.

"I'll look after you," I whispered. "I promise."

Probably half an hour later, a key clicked in the door. It opened, and Simon barreled down the hallway into the living room.

His eyes immediately went to the baby, and the tension in his face relaxed a little. "I was on my way home when you called," he said. "What happened? Is he okay?"

"He's fine."

He sat beside me on the couch. Worry lines were etched into his features. He looked older. "Where's your mom?"

I nodded toward the stairs. Simon bent down to kiss his baby on the forehead and then stared at me as if he wanted me to tell him what to do.

"Go." I ordered. I declared a silent truce with him. My mom needed him, and right now, so did I.

He broke out of his trance and got to his feet and slid off his shoes. "You think she's going to be okay?"

What the heck did I know? I was a seventeen-year-old kid. I nodded. "She'll be fine," I said to convince both of us.

He bolted up the stairs two by two and closed the bedroom door behind himself. My mom cried hysterically, but eventually she quieted down, and I heard the low murmur of their voices talking.

I focused on my brother, willing his tiny chest to keep moving up and down while he was blissfully unaware of the drama going on around him. I stood and took him to the playpen, where I placed his little sleeping body back inside and covered him with a blanket. My heart ached for him.

Simon finally slipped out of the bedroom and dragged himself down the stairs. I waited, my hand on my throat.

He plunked heavily on the couch beside me. "She's been acting weird all week. Your grandma thinks she's just being dramatic. I think she's in trouble."

I nodded. "Me too."

"God. I want my mom," he said, and then he leaned over and grabbed the phone book from the magazine rack beside the couch. "I'm calling the hospital. Screw your grandma."

I hid my shocked expression behind my hand and then listened while he spoke with a nurse and explained Mom's increasingly irrational behavior. Reality hit hard. There was something really wrong with her. Concern echoed in his voice, but I also heard his commitment to helping my mom with her mental well-being. He wasn't running away. He was dealing.

He sighed when he hung up, leaned back against the sofa, and breathed deeply in and out. I needed to hear what they'd said, but I dreaded hearing his voice telling me the facts.

"They think it's postpartum depression," he finally said, his chin dropping to his chest. "They want me to take her to the ER. They said she needs to see a psychiatrist, and that's the quickest way to get one."

My heart thumped. The room spun, but I focused on his face. "She's not crazy, is she?"

Simon scratched his head. "I don't know." His eyes welled up. "She's been talking about dying, and the baby and I being better off without her." He closed his eyes. His face crumpled as he tried to fight off tears. "I don't know what else to do."

"Go," I told him. "Take her. I'll stay. I'll look after the baby."

I tried not to ignore the overwhelming fact that I knew nothing about babies. I'd never even baby-sat in my life.

He rubbed at the short hair on his head. "It'll probably take hours at the ER."

"Go. I'll be fine."

"You sure you'll be okay?" He massaged his forehead, his expression uncertain.

"I can handle it. You have to take her. She needs to go. "

Upstairs Mom's bedroom door opened. Simon leaped to his feet as Mom shuffled down the hallway, peeked down the stairs, and then took a step toward us. Her hair was still dirty and messy, and she had on no makeup, but she'd put on an old pair of sweatpants and one of Simon's big T-shirts. Her face looked calmer, accepting of her fate.

"Jaz is great with the baby," she called out softly to Simon. "Better than I am."

"Mom," I said. "That's not true."

She took another step down. "I love him."

"I know," Simon said.

"No. I was talking to Jaz," she said softly.

"I know you love him," I said.

Her eyes watered. She wrapped her arms around herself. "You were right. I'm the worst mother in the world."

I remembered what I'd said to her at the restaurant. "Oh, Mom. You're not. I never meant that. I was just being awful, trying to hurt you. You're a good mom." I blushed. "You're sick. Go with Simon. I'll take care of the baby. It's okay. You need to get looked after too."

She grabbed the railing on the stairs and whimpered. "Everyone else always has to take care of my babies."

Simon bounded up the stairs, and when he reached her, she folded against him for support. He helped her down the stairs. Her pale, makeup-free face bothered me almost as much as her behavior. When they reached the bottom, she let go of Simon and tiptoed to the playpen.

"I'm sorry, baby," she whispered, stroking their son's fingers. "I love you. I do."

She wiped away her tears and struggled to gain control, and then she turned to me. "Joe," she said.

She glanced at Simon. He nodded.

"His name. Joseph Simon Peacock. Joe for Grandpa."

I wiped under my eyes as she gave me instructions on the proper way to change diapers and how often to feed him. Simon wrapped a coat over her shoulders and moved her toward the front door.

"Look after Joe," he told me.

"I will."

My mom shivered, and he led her away and left me all alone. In charge of my baby brother's life.

chapter eighteen

Simon walked through the front door hours later, waking me from a light sleep on the couch. He hurried to the playpen, bent down, and scooped up Joe, snuggling him close.

"Where's my mom?"

"I'll put him upstairs in his crib," Simon said. "And then we can talk about your mom."

"Leave him. I'll stay on the couch tonight. That way I can get up with him if he cries."

Simon shook his head. "No. That's not your job, Jaz. You've done so much already. I'm his dad. I get up with him. He'll sleep in his crib. I have a baby monitor."

I nodded, a little surprised. I'd kind of expected that he would let me be the one to look after Joe. Instead he was being totally responsible and dealing with things head-on.

"Is my mom okay?"

"She's been admitted. She's in good hands."

I bit my lip, waiting as Simon carried little Joe up the stairs to settle him in his room. A few minutes later, Simon returned carrying the baby monitor. He propped it on the coffee table and fell back on the couch, rubbing his eyes.

"They admitted her?" I asked again.

He nodded. "The doctors think it's severe postpartum depression. They're worried she might be suicidal. They're going to try to stabilize her with meds." He looked down at his hands. "They want to keep her in the psych ward for a few weeks."

I breathed out. "The psych ward? A few weeks?"

"It'll take a while for the medicine to start working, and they can monitor it there. She's terrified and she's horrified, but there's relief in her face too. You know? She's definitely not herself. She knows she needs help."

He stood up and looked around the room, and then he sat again, his face confused.

"She's embarrassed to admit she has a mental illness." He made quote marks in the air with his fingers. "But, she's so bad right now that she's willing to do anything to get better. She's really scared. For the baby."

I picked at my nails but didn't respond.

"It's an illness. Like diabetes or something. They have to treat it. The doctor said we shouldn't be ashamed of her, of what's happening to her. We want to make sure she gets better."

He jumped to his feet again and wandered into the kitchen.

"I called your grandma. She came to the hospital. I made her meet with the doctor. She's trying to digest the fact that your mom has a real illness and isn't just looking for a way out." He grabbed a glass from the cupboard and went to the sink to pour himself water. "Your grandma's trying. I'll give her that."

"Grandma's been kind of tough on her."

Simon nodded. "I know, but she talked to some nurses and they gave her material to read. She wants you to stay here tonight since it's late and to call her in the morning." He paused. "They gave your mom something to make her sleep. She hasn't slept in days." He blinked, dazed. "She needs sleep. No wonder she's so messed up. She hasn't slept."

He chugged back the water in one gulp.

"The doctor said it's part of the illness. Insomnia. He said it's all a part of it. The panic, feeling like she can't cope or can't handle the baby."

He put his glass on the counter. "They told me she'll get better, Jaz. She will get better."

"I looked it up on the Internet when you were gone." I'd googled her symptoms and was led straight to a page on postpartum depression.

I sighed. "I'm glad you took her to the hospital. Thanks."

"I should have known earlier. Man, I should have helped more when Joe was in the hospital," Simon said. "I thought she was doing okay. I should have known." He plunked down on the love seat opposite the couch. "I should have taken her in sooner."

He cradled his head in his hands.

My heart opened to him a little. "None of us knew. Grandma hasn't been helping much either. Or me." I hung my head. "I haven't been around. I've been kind of avoiding her."

Simon exhaled. "You're a good kid. This is a lot for you to handle."

I studied my nails again. He didn't know the whole truth of everything I'd been handling. His secret too. Him and Lacey.

"We're going to get her through this," Simon said, his voice choked with emotion and conviction. "She's going to be okay. She'll be okay."

He seemed so genuine. A tear slipped from my eyes and trailed wetly down my cheek. "Simon." I held my breath. "Do you love my mom?"

"What?" He glanced up. "Of course I do. She's the most important thing in the world to me. Her and Joe."

I studied the dark, rich color of his skin. He seemed so distraught. And sincere.

"And you too, kid. You're part of this too," he added.

I bit my lip and reached for my guitar charm. I'd hit him, and he'd kept it quiet. Probably to protect me. I needed to know if he meant it. If he'd be there for the long run. My mom was really sick, and I needed to know if he would be there. I took a deep breath and dropped my eyes.

"I won't ever tell her about what happened."

Simon stared at me, confused.

"About Lacey," I whispered. My heart pounded a melody of panic. "I know."

Simon's features froze. He sat up straighter. "What about Lacey?"

"I saw you," I said quietly. "At Marnie's. With Lacey."

Simon's forehead wrinkled. His brows creased together, but he stayed perfectly still, breathing in and out. I held my breath, waiting for him to deny it. To make an excuse.

Then he melted. His entire body drooped as if his bones had liquefied. His eyes glistened. He groaned and dropped his head.

"Oh, God. You saw me kissing her. Oh. God. No wonder. No wonder." His body shook as he fought back tears, swallowing and gasping for air.

He looked up at me, his brown eyes drenched with sadness and regret. "No wonder you belted me that day. Man. I'm so sorry. I didn't know. I didn't. I honestly thought you hated me because of your dad leaving. I didn't realize it was because of me."

Tears dripped down my cheeks.

He scratched at his head with both hands. "It was stupid, Jaz. So incredibly stupid. I would never fool around on your mom. That's something I promised myself when I was a kid. Not after the way my dad acted. I don't know how it happened. I was so drunk, and all of a sudden we were kissing, and then when I realized what the hell I was doing, I got out of there as fast as I could. I had no idea you saw."

I stared at him. "You got out of there?"

He rubbed his head and looked sick to his stomach.

"You didn't sleep with her?"

He did a double take. His face looked sincerely shocked.

"Sleep with her?"

He didn't. He wasn't lying. Why hadn't Lacey told me? I racked my brain, thinking about our conversations. I'd never come right out and asked her, and she probably didn't remember anyhow. Lacey's drinking was so bad she had blackouts all the time.

"I'm a jerk, but not that big of a jerk." Then he shook his head. "God. I never wanted to hurt your mom. Or you. You've got to know that. I was just freaked out when I found out she was pregnant, and I got stupidly drunk. Oh, man. I'm so sorry, Jaz. Your stupid friend of all people. I'm such a fucking idiot."

He clamped his hand over his mouth and his eyes widened.

"Your mom would kill me if she knew I just said 'fuck' in front of you."

We stared at each other for a second, both of us with eyes wide. The absurdity hit me first. I started to giggle and couldn't stop. Almost hysterically. Simon joined in, and for a moment we howled like lunatics. Tears streamed down both of our faces. The last thing my mom would be worried about right now was Simon swearing.

Simon wiped his eyes first, fighting for composure. He swallowed. The laughter disappeared.

"Now I understand why you've been so pissed with me. At McDonald's..." He swallowed and scratched at his head again. "I was going to tell your mom what I did, but she was so moody and down when she was pregnant, and then the baby came early and then..." He grabbed his head with both hands. "I didn't know what to do."

I held my breath. I didn't forgive him. Not completely. Not yet. He had some proving to do. But for now, he was here. Remorseful. Mom needed him, and maybe I did too.

And so I made the decision. For my mom. She couldn't do it herself. I had to think of her health and her baby. My brother. "Don't tell her," I said quietly.

Simon closed his eyes. "I have to."

"No," I said firmly. "You don't. The best thing right now is to forget it ever happened. Especially now. She's sick. The most important thing is to help her get better."

Simon didn't answer for a moment. "I didn't mean to involve you," he said, scratching at his head.

"Well, you did."

He looked up, and in his eyes, I saw his regret. His shame.

"I know," he said.

"It's done. So now do me a favor and don't tell her," I repeated.

He hung his head again, speaking to the carpet. "It was a horrible mistake, Jaz. I love your mom. I love our baby. I'll do anything to protect them. Anything. Nothing like that will ever happen again."

I stared at him, thoughts running through my head, and swallowed a lump. "Good."

The baby monitor crackled, and Joe began to chortle and cough.

We both shot to our feet.

"Sit." Simon smiled, a sad, tired effort. He started toward the stairs. "I've got him."

I bit my lip, holding in tears. "You're here to stay?"

His eyes glistened. "I am. I promise. I am."

I reached for my dangling charm, rubbing it between my fingers. "Okay," I said quietly.

And then I smiled. "But if you ever do something like that again, I swear I'll castrate you."

He winced as he put his hand on the stair railing. "Got it." He turned back. "This is what you were writing about, isn't it?" he asked. "Your song? I'm the one who betrayed you?"

I nodded.

He pressed his lips together and shook his head. "I really am sorry. And not just that I got caught."

He went up the stairs to comfort my brother. Tears dripped down my cheeks as I hugged myself. Some things just can't be undone. But he wasn't a horrible person. Not all the way through.

I didn't want to be either.

"I forgive you," I whispered. Maybe someday I would tell him in person.

chapter nineteen

I walked into Grinds clutching Jackson's hoodie close, inhaling his smell and trying to be brave. I checked behind the coffee counter. He was working. I slowly walked toward him. He glanced up and his eyes gave me a sense of his hostility, but I forced myself to keep moving. Mission. I had a mission. He deserved an apology. I planned to ask for his forgiveness. See if he could give me that, see if we could go back to being friends. It was all he'd wanted from me anyway. I'd take it. If he could forgive me. That part of the decision wasn't mine.

I thought about what I'd been rehearsing. I'd start with a joke. Jackson couldn't resist a laugh.

"Hey," I said. "What do you call a cow who's just given birth?"

He blinked without even cracking a smile. Remembering my resolve, I stood straighter. I wouldn't want to run from this.

"De-calf-inated."

His eyes didn't even sparkle.

"I'm sorry," I started to say, but he'd flipped on the espresso machine and nothing I said would be heard over the racket. I waited until the noise died down.

"I'm so sorry about the awful things I said," I told him when the machine went silent. I swallowed and took a deep breath. "I don't think you're a faker. I mean, it's not your fault you don't look biracial, and there's no way you should act, and you totally deserve sharing the heritage. I was just trying to hurt you. It was stupid. And immature and I didn't mean it."

He slowly drizzled chocolate over a coffee drink but didn't look up.

My cheeks warmed and I took a deep breath. "The thing is, I was embarrassed for, um, kissing you. And I just kind of popped when I found out you had a girlfriend. I mean, it's no excuse, but I'd been holding so many things in, and when I got mad at you, everything seemed to come to the surface and I went for your blood. It wasn't fair."

I waited but Jackson kept working, not looking at me. "I guess I read our relationship all wrong, and when I realized you had a girlfriend, it mortified me. See, I was kind of dumb, and I thought there might be something more than just friendship." My cheeks blazed but I made myself keep going. I'd practiced the speech in my mind a million times. "I'm stupid, and I lashed out at you to cover up my own humiliation. I didn't mean what I said. It's not true. None of it. I'm very sorry."

I understood a little of how Nathan had felt now. Why he'd lashed out at me. Lacey had said he had a thing for me, and it was unrequited just like me with Jackson. It hurt, but I wouldn't let that be an excuse to act like a total jerk.

Jackson lifted the coffee drink he was making and placed it on the counter. A woman stepped out from behind me, gave me a compassionate glance, and reached for her coffee. I forced myself to stay still and not run away in horror. The woman took her drink and left, but first she smiled at me with sympathy.

I took a deep breath. "I had a stupid crush on you, but I'm totally cool with being friends. I mean if you want…I mean, I won't expect anything more of you. But I'd like to be friends. If you can forgive me."

People did it all the time. Hung out with unreciprocated loves. Stayed friends. Jackson and I had so much in common, and I really liked talking with him.

I held out his hoodie. "Here. I brought this back."

"Hey, Jaz, long time no see."

I swiveled. Lacey stood behind me, her hands clasped in front of her.

"Hey, Lacey," I said, biting my lip and wishing she'd disappear. The girl had the worst timing.

Lacey squirmed on her feet as if she were nervous too. "I've been wanting to talk to you forever. Can I buy you a drink?"

I glanced at Jackson.

"You should sit with her. She needs to talk." Jackson said, and his expression was unreadable. "And keep the hoodie. I don't need it."

I swallowed my disappointment. I'd hoped for forgiveness, maybe even an offer of friendship, but I guess I'd gone too far. He wasn't going to give either. "Okay. Well. I'll see you around, maybe at school." At least I'd apologized. I'd tried. I was proud of myself for doing it, for making an effort to be more forgiving and open.

I turned to Lacey and made a show of checking my watch. I didn't want to spend too much time with her. "I guess we can sit and chat for a minute, but I can't stay long. I have to babysit my brother."

"Can I buy you a drink?" she repeated.

"Nope. I'm good."

"Something else?" Lacey shifted from foot to foot.

"Nope. I'm fine."

Her eyes filled with tears, and her face looked pained before she glanced down at her hands, studying her nails.

"Uh. You okay? You going to get something?"

"No."

"Okay, well, let's just sit then," I told her.

Lacey followed me to a table in the café and plunked down in the seat across from me. "I quit drinking," she blurted out as soon as her butt touched the chair.

I realized right away she didn't mean coffee.

"The thing is that I got really drunk a couple weeks ago and ended up in the hospital." She smiled sadly and wiped under her eyes. "It was pretty bad."

I reached for my charm bracelet and twisted it around. "Oh, Lacey. I didn't know. Are you okay?"

She smiled again, but it didn't light up her red eyes. "Yeah. I mean, I guess it's good. It made me see how bad off I was. You know, rock bottom and all that. Anyhow. That's not the part that I wanted to talk to you about. I hooked up with a guy." She bent her head and covered her mouth with her hand, covering a shy smile. "Not my usual hookup. I mean, he's a friend. He took me with him. To a meeting." She rolled her eyes. "AA."

She lifted her hand in a wave. "Hi, my name's Lacey, and I'm an alcoholic." She laughed self-consciously.

I blinked. "Wow. I mean, that's good, you know, if it's what you need."

"It is. I'm trying to deal with things better. You know, just like they say, one day at a time."

I nodded. "You've had it tough. I'm glad for you."

Her fingers snaked across the table, reaching for me. "I'm truly sorry. About what happened. You know, with Simon."

God. It seemed so long ago. A lifetime ago. I held her hand for a moment but then gently pulled away. "You know you didn't sleep with him, right?"

Her eyes lit up with relief. "I didn't?"

"No. He left. He didn't want to cheat on my mom. Not all the way."

"Thank God. I wasn't sure. You know my blackouts."

"I know," I told Lacey. "I'm glad you've stopped drinking."

"Me too." She cleared her throat. "And that's even better that it wasn't so bad because I kind of hoped we might, you know, be friends again someday. You're the best friend I ever had."

I stared down at the table before I looked up at her.

She sat up straighter, reading my expression and trying to hide her disappointment.

"No. I mean, I'm really trying to forgive you, Lace. You definitely aren't yourself when you drink. Drank. I know that. And I'm so sorry about what happened to you when you were younger." I chewed on my thumbnail.

"But..." I realized the truth and trusted myself to tell her. "I can forgive you, and I do. I forgive you, but I can't hang out with you. Not like before. I don't want to have to worry about awkward meetings with you and Simon or my mom finding out what happened. She couldn't handle it right now. I kind of have to look out for her."

I rubbed my guitar charm, hoping I was doing the right thing. I didn't want to tell Lacey about my mom's sickness. I wanted my mom to have her privacy until she started to get better. Someday, but not now.

Sometimes keeping secrets was the right thing to do.

Lacey's eyes glistened. "That's okay. I understand." She exhaled in a big puff. "I kind of hoped I could erase everything with an apology, but I guess 'sorry' can't fix some things."

"I'm sorry too, Lacey. I have to learn when to trust myself, when to believe in myself. I'm glad you're doing that too. You're being brave."

She smiled, but she wiped away a tear that ran down her cheek. "Thanks." She got to her feet. "I should get going. I have to work soon." She paused. "Is it cool if I keep working with your grandma? I really like working with those kids. It makes me feel...like I'm helping someone."

"Of course." I smiled at her. "You're totally going to do this, you know. Kick the drinking and feel better about yourself."

"Yeah." Lacey chewed her fake fingernail, a familiar old habit that I hadn't seen in a long time. "I guess I'll see you around. That's okay, right?"

We both stood, and I gave her a quick hug. She smiled, looking like a shadow of her old self. "Did you hear I got a new roommate?

A girl. She's in AA too. Nathan took off. He went to Phoenix after some girl he met online. Some girl from your high school dumped him and he was devastated, but he thinks this new girl is the one. He always thinks the girl he's into is the one." She laughed. "You know, believe it or not, I think Nathan is really looking for true love."

I attempted a smile. "I hope he finds it, then."

Lacey grinned. "Yeah, and you too. I'll see you around. Okay, Jazzy?"

I watched her leave, sad but also lightened by a sense of closure. She'd be okay without me, and I'd be okay too.

I glanced behind the coffee counter. Jackson had disappeared. With a sigh, I walked to the exit. I glanced behind me and then walked outside. I'd hoped for more from Jackson, but at least I'd said my piece. In a way it was kind of fitting that I couldn't forgive Lacey and he couldn't forgive me.

I started toward the sidewalk and then looked up and stopped dead in my tracks.

Jackson's car was parked illegally in front of the coffee shop, blocking the sidewalk. He was leaning against the car, his arms crossed in front, staring at me.

"Didn't you talk to Ashley?" he called out. "She was supposed to talk to you."

"Uh, I talked to her at school. She told me you were having lunch together."

"Yeah. But what else?"

"Nothing. She took off for an exam. I haven't seen her since."

Unsure of where to look or even which direction to walk in, I took a tentative step forward.

"She's not my girlfriend," he told me.

"Ashley? Um, yeah. I know." I frowned.

He laughed. "No. Carrie. She's not my girlfriend." He pushed a hand off his car and brushed back his long hair. "I broke up with her before I even moved to Tadita. It's been over for a long time."

"But she said she was your girlfriend."

"I know. She wouldn't let go. Carrie's got some issues. I told her we were breaking up before I went to rehab, but she hung on. Then Grams and I moved right away, and Carrie still had some of my stuff, and I still had some of hers. She was calling me a lot, and I felt sorry for her because of some of the stuff that had happened when I was doing drugs. She showed up unannounced the night you were at my place. Grams wanted me to take it easy on her. I had some amends to make. Sometimes I was a jerk. I was a different person then.

"She's going to rehab, but she's struggling and holding on to the past. I assured her we are over for good. I set her straight. Told her I was interested in someone else." He stepped toward me. "I gave her back all her stuff, and she went home."

"Oh."

"You owe me an apology."

"I said I was sorry," I said in a soft voice.

"Yeah. About calling me a faker. What about calling me a druggie? I'm not dealing anymore. Just so you know. That pissed me off. I haven't touched drugs since I left Whistler. I don't do them, and I don't deal them."

I groaned. "It's just that you got so many calls, and I heard you saying you had the stuff. It seemed so obvious…"

Jackson looked puzzled and then smacked his head with his hand. "Carrie. She was calling all the time using excuses like some CDs of hers I had and a couple of books. She used every excuse she could come up with to call. If I acted all mysterious and tried to cover it up, it was because I didn't want you to think she was my girlfriend. I should have just told you the truth."

I took a deep breath. More secrets that we should have told each other. "I'm sorry. For what I said…" I stopped, blushing.

Jackson grinned. "That I'm a stupid crush or a drug dealer? Or that I don't deserve to be black?"

"I can't believe I said any of that. Funny how I'm like everyone else, jumping to conclusions based on appearance."

I started full-on babbling but stopped when I saw his smile.

He took a step toward me. I clung to his hoodie and fought a desire to flee him and run to safety.

"Let's get one thing clear. You have never been just a friend to me." He stepped closer. "You didn't make a mistake when you kissed me. You surprised me, but I kissed you back with everything I had, and it was the best kiss of my life. It took all my friggin' will to pull away. I only did because otherwise I wouldn't have been able to stop myself. I thought it wasn't the right time for you.

"I've been waiting for it to be right. I didn't want to be, you know, a way of getting by, of coping with the bad stuff. I wanted to stay friends a while longer because you really needed one, and then I planned to bust out my moves later." He grinned, but his smile faded quickly. "But not telling you the truth about Carrie, not trusting you to understand was stupid, especially after you talked to me about Simon."

"I should have asked you about the dealing, instead of assuming. I guess I have to learn to trust people too. And myself. Even Simon."

"Simon?"

"I talked to him, and he did mess up that night like you said. He was embarrassed and guilty, and it was just a kiss, nothing more. I should have gone to him. Asked him about it."

He took another step and we faced each other, almost nose to nose. He leaned down and spoke right to my face. I smelled coffee on his breath but it was delicious. "You've intrigued me since the first time I saw you hauling around that guitar of yours at school. I mean, obviously I'm into guitars. And girls with guitars are a given. Especially since you're okay to look at and all." He grinned and reached out and pushed back a curl from my cheek. My stomach swooped.

"I watched you distance yourself from everyone and wondered what made you that way. I mean, I could tell you were biracial like me and I heard about you living with your grandma, but there was more. From the first day I laid eyes on you, there were sparks." He spread out his hand like each finger was a firecracker and fireworks were going off. "I couldn't figure out how to get to know you better at school since you didn't seem to talk to anyone, so I applied for a job at Grinds to meet you."

My mouth opened in surprise. "You did?"

"I wanted to get to know you. I didn't want to come on too strong or move too fast and scare you off. I didn't want to be all

'Hey, I'm biracial too, so let's hook up.' I wanted to tell you, but after I gave you a ride home that night, I saw you had a lot going on. I wanted you to get to know me and not the reputation. I have this messed-up past that follows me around now. I thought it might scare off a nice girl like you. And it did."

His phone rang and he cursed, but he pulled it from his pocket. He glanced at the number and smiled. "Oh, look. It's my drug dealer." He handed the phone to me. "Answer it."

I frowned, but he nodded and grinned. In a leap of faith, I clicked the phone on.

"Hello?"

"Jaz? Why are you on Jackson's phone?" Ashley's voice asked from the other end. I smiled and pulled the phone away from my ear. "Ashley?" I mouthed to Jackson. He lifted his shoulder and tilted his head innocently.

"Um. Why are you calling Jackson's phone?" I asked Ashley but kept an eye on him.

She ignored me. "Did you finally tell him you were an idiot?" she asked.

"Um. Maybe I am an idiot, but why are you calling Jackson's phone? Are you two all best friends now?" I fake-glowered at Jackson.

"Did you finally make up?" Ashley demanded. "Did you tell him you didn't mean what you said? That you're not as narrow-minded and stuck-up as you sounded?"

"Maybe." I smiled at Jackson.

"And he told you he's not with Carrie. That she's been stalking him."

"Well, he didn't say stalking."

"He should have. I met her, and she was kind of scary. Anyway, forget her. You are with Jackson! That is awesome. We are so going on a double date with Marnie," Ashley said. "The four of us. She'll be so happy. Jackson has been killing us with his misery."

"Jackson has been hanging out with you *and* Marnie?"

Jackson reached over and took the phone from my ear. "Quit giving away my secrets," he said to Ashley. "Jaz and I need to talk." He grinned at me and told Ashley we were busy and we'd talk to her later and hung up the phone.

"So you're all best buds with Ashley now?" I asked when he clicked his phone off.

He smiled. "You know I can't resist lesbians."

I punched him in the arm. "And she can't resist criminals."

He wrapped his arms around me and I buried my head in his chest, feeling shy. I inhaled the same scent that still lingered on his hoodie, the smell of him. Of boy. Not bad boy, not good, just boy. I didn't want to move out of his arms.

"So Ashley is happy," he said. "And planning double dates?"

"She'll dye her hair rainbow colors to celebrate," I said to his chest.

Jackson stepped back and gently took me by the shoulders and moved me in front of him. He lifted my chin with his finger. My skin tingled under his touch.

"I'll wait if you need time," he said. "But I want to be more than your friend."

"There's no waiting." I smiled and then groaned. "I'm so sorry about everything I said to hurt you."

He leaned down and whispered in my ear. "I forgive you."

"My life is still very messy," I warned.

"I'm okay with messy."

"My mom is sick," I told him. "Postpartum depression. She's in the hospital. Simon and Joe need my help."

"Joe?"

I grinned. "My brother. They finally named him. After my grandpa."

He nodded. "That's cool. So you'll be helping out, right? Things are better with you and Simon?"

"Yeah. They need me."

"Is she going to be okay?"

I shrugged, wishing I could be certain. "I hope so."

Jackson reached down and took the hoodie from my hands. I watched as he unraveled it and then gently pulled it over my head. I poked my arms through the sleeves, the first time I'd ever worn it properly on my body.

He reached for my hand and tugged on it. "Hey. Come on. I'm parked illegally here. Can I take you somewhere?"

"You know anything about babies?"

He looked a little frightened, and I laughed. "I could use some help babysitting in an hour. I won't make you change diapers, but I want to be there for my family. I promised Simon I'd look after Joe. So he could visit Mom. You could keep me company."

He twirled his hoop earring. "Sure. But later you've got to come and meet my grandma. She's going to eat you up."

A spark of anticipation ignited in my chest. I wanted to meet her even though it terrified me. "I hope so. My grandma already called you handsome and polite."

"She has impeccable taste." He chuckled. "You have no idea what you're getting into with Grams."

I shrugged off my nerves. "Piece of cake." I was lying. But it wasn't a bad lie.

He grinned at me. "Whatever, right?"

"Yeah," I said, grinning wider. "Whatever."

He took my hand. I threw my head back and laughed, and the sound that rolled out from deep inside me echoed loudly in the air between us.

And then Jackson leaned forward and kissed me.

chapter twenty

My knees pressed against each other, and swoops of anxiety roller-coastered around my insides, making me even more unsteady on my shaky feet. Water dripped down my face.

"Are you okay?" Ashley asked from behind me. I turned to look at her.

Her wet hair was slicked back, the colored tips dripping with water. She looked so much stronger and more powerful in her bathing suit. Her arms were rounded with muscles, her shoulders broad. She was so comfortable and nonchalant in her swimsuit that I felt a little better about prancing around half naked myself. Water from the locker-room showers flowed around her feet.

"Fine," I said. "I'm fine."

She held out her hand. "Come on. You're done showering."

"It's so freezing," I complained and wrapped my arms around my waist.

"You'll get used to it once you're in the water, trust me."

"Trust you," I grumbled and reached for the faucet and turned the shower off.

I followed her out of the women's locker room and stepped onto the pool deck. The blue water in the pool mocked me as the scent of chlorine filled my nose. The smell brought back memories. I straightened my back and pulled the back of my bathing suit down, making sure it covered my butt.

Ashley said hi to the lifeguard and walked over to the shallow end of the pool. I didn't follow her. I glanced over at the small viewing area. Jackson stood up and waved. He held Joe up, but Joe was curled up, fast asleep.

So much for my little brother witnessing my first step back in the pool.

"Come on," Ashley called. "We've only got a half hour until my practice."

I took a tiny step forward toward the pool.

acknowledgments

Many people gave me eyes and thoughts on this book, which evolved and changed over time, but my first thanks has to be to Leah Hultenschmidt, my lovely editor at Sourcebooks, for choosing to bring Jaz to life and then giving me guidance to help Jaz and her friends become more alive.

I also need to thank my wonderful agent, Jill Corcoran, and lovely folks at Sourcebooks like Aubrey Poole, Kelly Barrales-Saylor, Kay Mitchell, Kristin Zelazko, and the sales and marketing people. (And all the others behind the scenes who I haven't had a chance to meet or thank personally yet.) Teen Fire rocks!

To Bethany Hegedus, the best friend I've never met, for taking time to go through the story line by line and helping me see things I missed. And also for our great chats and pep talks over the years. I truly treasure you!

Thanks also to readers who gave me great feedback including Robin Graf Prehn, Ronni Selzer, Pamela Yaye, and Barbara Etlin.

And though this book is about Jaz, close to my heart is her mother's experience with postpartum depression. I want to thank Dr. Diana Turner in Calgary for helping me believe I was going to be all right when I didn't know if I would be.

Praise for *I'm Not Her* by Janet Gurtler

"Subtle, believable, and satisfying...[a] quick and heartbreaking read"
—School Library Journal

Chicago Tribune
Summer Reading Pick

"Reminiscent of Judy Blume"
—RT Book Reviews, 4.5 stars

"Cute and quirky, with sentimentality **reminiscent of Judy Blume**, this is a book for the keeper shelf—one that readers will devour again and again!"

—*RT Book Reviews*, 4.5 stars

"Rich in characterization, Gurtler's novel wrestles with some serious issues and explores different means of coping (or escaping) yet manages not to be overwhelming or bleak. **Just right for fans of Sarah Dessen and Jodi Picoult**, this is a strong debut."

—*Booklist*

"**Subtle, believable, and satisfying.** The author seamlessly develops complexity in all of the characters... This **quick and heartbreaking read** realistically shows how one person's illness affects an entire community."

—*School Library Journal*

"A story that is **nothing but completely real**... **[You] will find yourself inspired**."

—*Girl's Life*

"Gurtler's writing unfurls with the exquisite grace of a flower. Readers will cheer Tess's triumphant awakening as she blooms in the shade of insecurity, family tragedy, and sibling rivalry to discover a strength and beauty all her own."

—Sarah Ockler, bestselling author of *Fixing Delilah* and *Twenty Boy Summer*

"This is one **gripping, heartfelt story about sisters and the bond that holds them together**."

—*YABooksCentral*

"**Will both make you smile and break your heart**...I couldn't put it down."

—*Rex Robot Reviews*

"The strength of sisterhood speaks volumes...**A great story about love, loss and the lengths one will go to when facing death**."

—*The Page Turners*

"This book was beautiful—almost poetic in a way. I would definitely recommend it—**especially to fans of Sarah Ockler and Gail Forman**."

—*I Like These Books*

"**A powerful, emotional story...a book everyone can relate to**."

—*My Words Ate Me*

"Just right for fans of Sarah Dessen and Jodi Picoult"
—*Booklist*

"**An emotionally riveting debut novel and I have no doubt it will resonate deeply with readers...This is a wonderful book that readers of all ages will take to heart**."

—*Bookfinds*

L.A. Times
Summer Reading Pick

about the author

Janet Gurtler lives in Calgary, Canada, deliciously close to the Canadian Rockies, with her husband, son, and the memories of a sweet little dog named Meeko. Janet does not live in an igloo or play hockey, but she does love maple syrup and says "eh" a lot.